Foresight

Beginning's End Series, Volume 4

W.J. May

Published by Dark Shadow Publishing, 2022.

BEGINNING'S END SERIES

FORESIGHT

USA Today Bestselling Author

W.J. MAY

1

BEGINNING'S END SERIES
FORE SIGHT
USA TODAY BESTSELLING AUTHOR
W. J. MAY

Have You Read the C.o.K Series?

The Chronicles of Kerrigan
Book I - *Rae of Hope* is FREE!

BOOK TRAILER:

http://www.youtube.com/watch?v=gILAwXxx8MU

How hard do you have to shake the family tree to find the truth about the past?

Fifteen year-old Rae Kerrigan never really knew her family's history. Her mother and father died when she was young and it is only when she accepts a scholarship to the prestigious Guilder Boarding School in England that a mysterious family secret is revealed.

Will the sins of the father be the sins of the daughter?

As Rae struggles with new friends, a new school and a star-struck forbidden love, she must also face the ultimate challenge: receive a tattoo on her sixteenth birthday with specific powers that may bind her to an unspeakable darkness. It's up to Rae to undo the dark evil in her family's past and have a ray of hope for her future.

Find W.J. May

Website:
https://www.wjmaybooks.com
Facebook:
https://www.facebook.com/pages/Author-WJ-May-FAN-PAGE/
141170442608149
Newsletter:
SIGN UP FOR W.J. May's Newsletter to find out about new releases,
updates, cover reveals and even freebies!
https://www.wjmaybooks.com/subscribe

Foresight Blurb:

USA Today Bestselling author, W.J. May, continues the highly anticipated best-selling YA/NA series about love, betrayal, magic and fantasy.

Learn to fight—it is the only option...

How long can you hold back the tide?

When Kiera and her friends reach the hollow, they think they're finally going to get the answers they so desperately seek. How can they kill a dragon? How can they even find it? But instead of answers, they're left with riddles and even more questions.

Instead of returning to civilization, instead of rallying more people to their side, the friends make a decision that sets them upon an even more dangerous quest than the one they were on before.

They're going after the dragon themselves.

The will is strong, but the journey is fraught with peril and their newfound fellowship isn't as stable as it seemed. The world is changing and those turbulent forces are getting stronger every day.

How do you hunt such a monster? What can you do if you find it?

One way or another, they're about to find out.

BE CAREFUL WHO YOU trust. **Even the devil was once an angel.**

BEGINNINGS CURIOSITY SCRUTINY FORESIGHT DISAVOW TRICKERY
WISDOM DECREE INFLUENCE PREVAIL DIGNIFIED HONORED

Beginning's End Series

Beginnings
Curiosity
Scrutiny
Foresight
Disavow
Trickery
Wisdom
Decree
Influence
Prevail
Dignified
Honored

The Queen's Alpha Series

Eternal

Everlasting

Unceasing

Evermore

Forever

Boundless

Prophecy

Protected

Foretelling

Revelation

Betrayal

Resolved

The Omega Queen Series

Discipline
Bravery
Courage
Conquer
Strength
Validation
Approval
Blessing
Balance
Grievance
Enchanted
Gratified

Prologue

The fae's breathing was low and even. It seemed almost a shame to disturb him.

The day had been racing, but now all was still—caught in the misty golds between late afternoon and the crest of twilight. It seemed for anyone watching, as if the world itself was taking a breath, finished with one task and slow to begin another. A summer breeze idled along the soft grasses of the meadow, smoothing them first one way, then another. The slumbering birds tucked into a lacework of branches, too high and quiet for anyone to see.

The vampire crept ever-closer, struck with a reverence that silenced his footsteps and captured his breath.

Had he been the laughing type, he might have laughed then. There was something preposterous about it, like stumbling upon a painting someone careless had left in the grass. The immortal was stretched in perfect recline, drifting in and out of dreams, every line of him curving gently against the ground, as if he'd been made to complete just that part. His sunswept hair fanned loose in a halo and his lashes casted slanting shadows across his cheeks, while his body was cast in a celestial glow. The sun didn't bear down upon him the way it did so many others. It caressed him instead—warming his features and illuminating from within, so all that light seemed almost to spill right out of him.

To leave his presence, was to step into shadow. Venture close enough, that warmth was catching.

The vampire was standing very close. About to get closer still.

He took a step, then froze—staring as though lost in a dream. The fair folk were a dangerous enemy, at times even more lethal than his own kin. He carried no illusions of this, and yet, he could not help but approach. There was a slight hitch in breathing, but otherwise, the fae didn't stir. His quiver and bow were lying in the grass beside him, well-used but polished to a shine. The vampire edged them carefully away, then knelt down beside him.

He smiled then. It was impossible not to smile.

His people were of the shadows, the farthest thing from all that light. Never would he be permitted to live alongside one of these creatures. To wander the forest, share a meal. Or even know his name. The sun and the stars, the laws of nature had decreed it so. But then why the temptation? Why make them so utterly impossible to ignore?

Had he the control, he might have tried to defy those laws. Striking an acquaintance with this ethereal creature, running a finger along his brow, trying to coax a breathtaking smile.

But the mastery eluded him. And beneath that sunlit skin lay the greatest treasure of all.

He lashed out with the speed of a snake, striking the fae across the temple and dazing him before he had a chance to open his eyes. There was a quiet gasp as his pulse quickened. A touch of pain rippled across his face.

Then came the blood. It was always going to be the blood.

A pair of fangs sank into the fae's neck the moment he opened his eyes, drawing a look of panic and a soft cry. His arms came up of their own accord, trying to dislodge the vampire as his legs began scrambling, but there was little that could be done. Before a full minute had passed, his famed strength was already beginning to falter—draining like liquid gold into the vampire's thirsty mouth.

"Mios..."

It was the only word the vampire could identify, and in a moment of dizzied intoxication, he actually pulled back to stare at his prize. What he saw changed everything. There wasn't any fear—that was what he'd been expecting. The shock had already faded, and there wasn't any anger or surprise. If anything, the fae looked...melancholy.

There was something tragic about it. To see such sadness on such a beautiful face.

"Mios," the vampire repeated, and the word felt unfamiliar on his tongue. "What does it mean?"

The fae gazed up at him, slipping in and out of consciousness.

He didn't answer, perhaps he couldn't. He merely lifted a trembling hand, placing it in the center of the vampire's chest. Their eyes met, and in that suspended moment, there was a profound shifting, as if the vampire's very rooting had been torn from the ground and planted someplace else.

He stared the way one looked at oceans and constellations. He stared the way one looked at angels and glimpses of the divine, understanding the existential draw of such wonders for the first time.

He stared as if it was his first and only sunrise, watching the celestial light flicker in those eternal eyes.

There was a quiet exhale of breath and the fae died in his arms, blinking out like a candle caught in the breeze. The vampire held him for what felt like an eternity, then closed his eyes and lay him gently in the grass.

The sun had set, and the shadows had come. His relentless tormentors, chasing him from one night to the next. For the space of a heartbeat, he had cast off their heavy burden, escaping into a fleeting moment of light.

But such freedom could never last. They would chase him much further.

He wasn't sure they would never stop.

Chapter 1

"What are you reading?"

Kiera startled, then closed her book—glancing up with a forced smile as Jesse strode back down the path. They were in a brief respite of a never-ending hike, a moment of unexpected calm as the immortal members of their party scouted further ahead for the best route through the forest.

"It's nothing," she said quickly, tucking her hair behind her ears, "a poem written about a fae and a vampire. Kind of heartbreaking stuff, really."

Kind of striking too close to home.

His face brightened with a teasing smile.

"There is poetry about such things?" he quipped, tossing an apple into her hands and taking a bite of another. "Nothing too lyrical, I hope. I'd imagine it to be more of a limerick. There once was a fae from Ardell, who gathered his friends by a well. A vampire walked by, they took out their knives, and sent that fool straight back to—"

There was a rustling of leaves, as both immortals appeared in the clearing.

They had come from separate directions, having wandered down opposite sides of the wooded slope, but arrived back at precisely the same time. Evander's eyes went as always for Eden, while the fae greeted his companions with a sparkling smile.

"What are you speaking about?" he asked brightly. "I could have sworn I heard a rhyme."

They froze a moment, then Kiera slid the book into her pack.

"Nothing."

"Nothing."

Upon leaving the hollow just a few days before, the journey facing the friends had been wildly uncertain. While they had already travelled a perilous road searching for answers, there was always meant to be an end to it. A collection of more people, with more weapons, and more strength to add to their own. There was always meant to be a solution, a well-earned finish to their precarious isolation, as they folded themselves into the waves of others flooding to their cause. That had been the *intent*. But their savior had provided nothing but riddles and vague promises of despair.

You cannot kill a dragon. You need a dragon to kill a dragon.

Many times as the sun beat down on her shoulders, Kiera had remembered Marrow's easy smiles with a pang of true hatred—pressing her lips together and grinding her teeth.

It was death, he offered. Nothing more.

The only reason they were still trudging through the forest, still heading towards the grisly unknown, was that someone needed to do it. And despite being rather wickedly removed from the situation, the fates had provided the smallest glimmer of hope.

Or maybe the fates had nothing to do with it. Maybe it was the sheer will of a fae.

"Come on—tell me," Eden insisted, stealing the shifter's apple and taking a large bite for himself. "I always include the pair of you in my own compositions."

"And I wish you wouldn't," Jesse replied crossly, swiping for it. "As I've said many times."

When he missed the first time, he tried a second. When Eden held it out of reach, eyeing him with a devilish grin, he vaulted off a nearby poplar and attacked the fae from behind.

Kiera watched their antics with a faint smile.

There had been no hiding the fae's excitement since they'd left the hollow. Unlike the rest of his companions, who tread carefully and glanced over their shoulders with every step, the man acted as though he'd been unleashed—bounding from one place to another, casting those sparkling eyes to the horizon, and lifting the others' spirits with every liberated breath.

It was nothing strange to him, chasing after monsters with nothing but the sun on his cheeks and the bow on his back. He'd dreamt of nothing else since he was just a boy.

"Were you able to find anything?" Evander finally prompted, arms folded across his chest.

He, too, had been watching the shifter and the fae attack each other, but held back with his usual reserve. There had scarcely been a moment since they'd left the hollow, when he *hadn't* been watching the fae. Always with the same silent worry, always with his eyes flickering to the clouds.

The only solace he seemed to find was his personal invitation to join the fellowship.

"Sorry?"

Eden detached himself with a tousled grin, still clinging to the stolen apple. Fresh blood had been drawn and the poplar had not survived the assault, but the fruit remained in his hands.

The vampire stole a lingering glance before pursing his lips and trying again. "Did you find a better way down the mountain?"

"Oh—right." The fae tossed him the apple. "Yes, there's a decent path that winds along the ravine we spotted earlier. There's a stream that transects one part, but it's shallow enough to easily cross. We could reach it in a few days."

Evander stared a moment longer before looking into his hands. "Why did you give me this?"

Eden's lips curved in a sly smile. "Because then I win."

Kiera cast a glance between them before letting out a snort of laughter.

It was an unlucky fool who would dare to retrieve their prize from the hands of a vampire. From the varied looks on the faces around her, the others were coming to realize this as well.

Jesse backed away with a sullen glare, while Evander froze in shock.

He continued staring at the fruit, then lifted his eyes to where the fae was patching a hole they'd discovered in the tent—whistling ancient victory tunes under his breath. There were many sides to such a creature, and he was coming to learn them all. The cheerful warrior, the restless dreamer. The immortal guardian, determined to embrace the potential of each new day.

But this new version? This mischievous prankster?

The vampire was all the more besotted by him.

He hesitated a moment, then joined him silently by the tent.

Without seeming to think about it, he picked up the thread the fae had been holding, pulling the canvas taut. Without seeming to think about it, the fae made a space, knotting the other side.

"I wanted to thank you," he said softly.

Eden glanced up in surprise. "For what?"

The vampire kept his eyes on the tent. "For what you said back at the hollow. That you wished for me to come along." His fingers stilled and his cheeks burned in the fading light. "I wish to stay, for however long you will have me."

A quiet hush fell over the campsite as their eyes met across the tent.

A strange series of emotions passed across the fae's face, too quickly to make sense of any of them. They rose and fell one after another, like waves cresting upon a tide.

In the end, he was simply blank.

"I'm glad to hear it. We could use the help."

He paced into the twilight without another word, pausing only to give Evander a friendly clap on the arm. It was for the best that he was facing, as always, towards the horizon.

He never had to see the look on the vampire's face.

IT FELT GOOD TO BE getting back to normal. A suicidal mission with astronomical odds. A simple stew beside a crackling campfire. Only there was nothing normal about it.

That night, something special had transpired.

"Seven hells!" Jesse stepped out from the curtain of trees, a sprig of freshly picked rosemary in his hands. "Did you actually cook something edible?"

Kiera flashed him a withering look, but couldn't in good conscience disagree. The friends had spent many tenuous nights chewing what she'd claimed to be root vegetables. While the fae made his opinion well known, the shifter had never offered a word of complaint.

"It's my own creation," she answered daintily, stirring around in the bubbling caldron. "The working title is Kiera's Wilderness Chowder, but I'm open to other suggestions."

He came up behind her, pressing a kiss to her cheek.

"Seriously, that smells amazing. And here I was going to smother it in this." He gave the rosemary a twirl before tossing it over his shoulder. "I'll find us some bowls."

The packs were already inside the tent, but he found the correct one quickly—rifling around inside for a brief moment before returning with everything they might need.

"You're just hungry," Evander said quietly, watching from the other side of the fire. He hadn't spoken much since the fae's casual dismissal. But he was watching the same as always, those dark eyes reflecting the dancing flames. "We were in that man's house for three days."

The stew was instantly forgotten, as the others turned to him in shock.

"Three days?" Kiera repeated in bewilderment. "What are you talking about?"

The vampire lifted his shoulders in a shrug.

"Time seems to move differently in such places. I thought you knew."

Seven hells!

In a flash, her mind replayed every second—trying to understand how it could have happened, trying to reconcile the shift. It had been afternoon when they arrived, and afternoon when they left. They could see the sun outside the window each moment. And yet...?

Eden tilted his head curiously, catching his gaze across the fire. "How did *you* know?"

Not for a moment did he question it was true. Despite whatever troubling undercurrents might plague them, he trusted the vampire implicitly, in a way he didn't even trust his own friends.

Must be an immortal thing.

Evander shrugged again, though for the first time, he seemed reluctant to meet the fae's gaze. "I felt it when we left, saw the shifting of the moon that night. Could you not sense it?"

The fae shook his head in silence, wondering why that might be.

"Three days," Kiera muttered indignantly, feeling strangely offended to have been robbed of the time. "Thank the gods we didn't stay for beets."

Jesse settled down beside her, placing a bowl in her hands. "Since we're finally speaking of the hollow," he began slowly, throwing the others a cautious glance, "I have a question about Marrow..."

Kiera nodded knowingly. "Why so tall?"

"Alright, two questions."

Eden rolled his eyes. "What is it, Jess?"

Perhaps the fae was hoping for some valid curiosity, an enlightened insight, that would lead to a thoughtful conversation, that might in turn lead to something else. But if that was what he'd been expecting, he was sadly mistaken. Because the shifter had his mind on something else.

"Evander...would you fight him?"

Kiera let out a breath of laughter, while the vampire glanced up in surprise. Eden stretched out his legs with an exasperated grin, though he seemed genuinely curious to know the answer.

"Would I fight him?" the vampire repeated slowly. He weighed the question a moment before his eyes suddenly cooled. "I am not your gauge for all things dangerous."

Jesse flashed a mischievous grin while Kiera answered apologetically.

"You kind of are."

"Let him be," Eden instructed.

"I'm just asking—"

"I would never wish to fight him," Evander interrupted, stopping the conversation in its tracks. "He is…different. It would never cross my mind."

It was quiet for a moment, as all four of them considered this—staring into the crackling flames and replaying the fateful encounter in their minds. To be perfectly honest, they'd all taken great pains *not* to think about Marrow since leaving the cottage. The business with the dragon was unsettling enough—as was his casual instruction to consult the dead—but it was those moments immediately after, when he'd taken each of them aside in turn.

Those were the moments that lingered, festering like a burn.

The fire crackled in between them, popping and hissing as the logs glowed with heat. Three spoons scraped quietly against bowls. Four people silently asked themselves the same questions.

Then Jesse lifted his eyes. "But if you *had* to fight—"

"Eat your soup."

A spattering of laughter broke the tension, as the friends settled back once again, content to leave those troublesome queries for another day. The bowls were refilled, as the caldron was quickly emptied. The vampire was right, their bodies were still playing catchup. They just hadn't known why.

"You're not even tempted?" Kiera asked with a smile, wafting it towards him.

He turned his head stiffly, taking in a breath of clean air. "I can't begin to tell you how much I'm *not* tempted."

"Don't take it personally, love." Jesse pushed to his feet with a grin, stretching his arms above his head. "It's one of your best. I couldn't find a single bone in mine."

Kiera started to smile, then flashed him a quick look.

Love.

Since the night of their fateful reading lesson, a great many affections and endearments had slipped into their vocabulary. But that one was quite different. That one was new.

"That's, uh…that's good. About the bones, I mean."

Eden's eyes drifted between them. Evander couldn't physically have cared less. The only one who remained oblivious was the shifter himself. He yawned widely, then headed for the tent.

"I vote the fae keeps first watch, seeing as this disaster was his idea and all of us will likely be killed for it. The rest of us should savor the memories and dream while we still can."

Charming.

He flashed a sweet smile and offered Kiera his hand. "We'll see you in the morning."

Eden nodded indulgently as the two headed to bed, too openly excited to take offense. He, too, had been contemplating what he now considered a rather fortuitous turn of events. It took him a moment to notice the one person who made no attempt to go inside.

"Why don't I just take the watch?" Evander asked quietly. "I'll be here anyway."

The fae's eyes flashed up as the others paused by the door.

"No, that's—"

But it was too late. The vampire was already gone.

NEEDLESS TO SAY, IT wasn't the easiest of nights.

The silent argument was already brewing as the three companions settled down to sleep as they always did. And though it came as no surprise, not everyone was one the same side.

"Are we really going to keep doing this?" Kiera demanded as soon as the others had lain down, folding her arms tight across her chest. "Making him sleep outside like some kind of animal?"

It had bothered her the first night after the hollow. She'd almost been moved to speak in the two nights since. But for whatever reason, that evening had proven the final straw.

"We slept together on the boat," she reminded them before anyone could answer. "Nothing happened. Nothing even *started* to happen. We're trusting him with our safety right now, making him keep watch. But we still won't let him sleep with us in the tent?"

The men shared a look, neither wanting to speak first.

"There's isn't any room—" Jesse began tentatively.

"After he saved us from those monsters," she interrupted frankly. "After he saved me from the river. After he volunteered to journey into the unknown and help us find the dragon. After all of that, you're *still* going to make him sleep outside?"

"He can hear you," Jesse mouthed, pointing to his ear.

She let out a frustrated sigh. "Eden, back me up."

The fae pointed to his ear as well. He simply used a different finger.

While he'd asked himself the same question many times, considering whether he should sleep outside in a show of solidarity, he didn't appreciate others asking it now. The same way a part of him had been strangely anxious when Jesse had given his approval to allow the vampire to travel alongside them. The same way all words had failed him, when they were standing by the fire.

"You would truly feel comfortable?" Jesse asked quietly, looking at her in surprise. He'd been right about there not being any room—the three friends were pressed against one another as it was. "You would truly be able to sleep with him so close?"

Probably not.

"Of course I would," she answered stiffly. "And I want you both to consider it. It's not fair that we ask him to take the same risks without offering the same comfort in return."

Jesse regarded her a moment before softening with a faint smile.

"The same comfort, huh?" His eyes flickered ever so briefly to Eden. "If that's really the way you feel, I'd be willing to consider it. I'm just not sure how comfortable we all wish him to be."

The fae said nothing in reply. He merely rolled over and pretended to sleep.

AS IT TURNED OUT, KIERA wasn't able to sleep that night anyway. She tossed and turned for a while, unable to get comfortable, before finally opening her eyes and staring around the tent.

It was after midnight and Eden was already on watch, prowling in the darkness somewhere with a bow at his side. But Jesse was still nestled right up against her. One arm was flung around her waist and his dark hair spilled across their shared blanket, fluttering with each shallow breath.

She smiled in spite of herself, staring from just inches away.

Love.

It was probably unintentional. It was probably just a pet name. If she racked her brain, she could probably remember a time that Eden had said the same thing. So why did it feel so different? Why did she remember the exact tone of his voice? Why did she keep playing it back in her mind?

She lifted the tip of her finger, tracing it along his lips.

It wasn't the easiest time to be thinking about such things, and yet, there was something quite natural about it as well. Something that defied their circumstance and made her think about only the good things—as if the mere sight of him made all the rest of the world simply fade away.

Perhaps it was merely their unsteady position. For the last few months, they'd been roaming the wilderness with nowhere to lean except on each other. Or perhaps it was something different.

Perhaps it was that he was *exactly* the person she would have chosen for herself.

With a surge of mischief, she leaned a little closer—wondering if he'd wake up with a soft kiss. Then a sudden pain shot down her leg and she reached between them, digging into her pocket.

Her hand came up with a stone.

It looked as lovely then, as it had hanging in Marrow's window—that clear blue somehow untouched by the shadows of night. She rolled onto her back, holding it thoughtfully above her head. There hadn't been a moment since they'd left when she hadn't been touching it. Her fingers found it with each passing step, with each mountain trail, turning it absentmindedly in her cloak.

Why did he give it to me? she wondered, examining it anew. *Why did he have it in the first place?*

A sudden wave of restlessness swept over her, and before she stopped to consider what she was doing, she eased free of Jesse's arm and slipped quietly outside the tent.

The moon was still hanging overhead, but its light was already fading—brightening into the soft pinks and brimming golds of a new dawn. She paused at the remains of the fire, nothing more than smoldering embers, and saw Evander wrapped in a blanket just a few paces beyond. His eyes were closed and that lovely face was completely relaxed, making him look younger than she'd seen.

So vampires DO sleep.

She smiled to herself, wandering away from the camp and into the trees.

Such a thing usually wasn't permitted, but those rules had eased somewhat with the addition of a vampire. A great many things had eased. Strange, given the tension of his arrival.

The ferns parted with a quiet rustle as she waded through the middle, rubbing the stone absentmindedly in her pocket, as she considered the poem she'd read earlier.

Was Jesse right? Was there an inevitable conclusion to such a thing? Or were the forces that had brought them together, greater than the ones that threatened to tear them apart?

There are exceptions to every rule, why not something like this?

She chewed pensively on her lips, breathing in the clean night air.

Why couldn't a fae make peace with a—

Something hard smacked into her face and she came to an abrupt stop—rubbing painfully at her nose and lifting her eyes to see what she'd run into. They kept lifting. And kept lifting.

Until finally, they reached the top.

Seven hells.

She swallowed hard, as the stone went limp in her hand.

This is why we don't wander after dark.

Chapter 2

"Eden?"

Kiera froze where she was standing, gazing upward like a silver-lit sapling, trembling in the breeze. Her arms and legs had gone numb the second her eyes made sense of what was happening.

A second after that, her brain presented a muddled assessment.

That is a cave troll.

She couldn't tell you how she knew it for certain. The only point of reference she had were the poorly-drawn illustrations from her childhood books. No one really knew what a cave troll looked like, because no one who'd ever encountered one had survived to bring back the tale. They were so far down on the list of peripheral possibilities, it almost failed to register—as if when her eyes swept the forest, they didn't see the hulking giant, but a blank space where it stood.

She whispered again into the forest, her voice lost in the shadows. "Eden?"

In hindsight, she probably should have called for the vampire. Not only were his senses unparalleled, but he was sleeping outside the tent. Jesse was another logical option, given that he could change into a lupine predator at the drop of a hat. There were a lot of things she probably should have done in hindsight. But when her lips opened, she found herself calling for the fae.

It was a childish reaction, but this was a monster from every childhood dream. The one that leaped with ready hands from the shadows. The one that could appear perfectly invisible, except for its eyes and its teeth. Two legs planted in the ground before her, coated in mottled skin and thick as an evergreen. The most unfortunate seamstress in the realm had constructed some type of loincloth, while the rest of its body seemed to stretch in every direction—bulging with muscles and curled into an inevitable fist. She couldn't quite make out the top of it, the lines were lost in the skyline, but she took that observation by itself to be quite a terrible sign.

That's probably the way everyone feels...the moment before they die.

She shuddered involuntarily, on the verge of blacking out. The only reason she wasn't dead already, was that the creature itself couldn't seem to get over the shock. It was staring at her with a crease down the middle of its forehead, the way wild animals avoided those that had gone mad.

Her eyes snapped shut as it leaned closer, leaving the fading warmth of twin tears streaking down her cheeks. The must of rotted breath washed over her, plastering her hair to her neck.

"Eden...*please.*"

It must have been nothing more than imagination, but she felt as though she heard him coming—turning his head somewhere else in the forest, as her voice drifted through the trees.

He stepped into the clearing a moment later, freezing shock-white.

His lips parted, but there wasn't anything to say. It was standing right there. She was standing right beside it. If she reached out a finger, it would touch that putrid flesh.

How?

"I walked into it," she whispered, breaking the silence.

The fae turned those eyes to her. "You walked into it?"

She swallowed a hard lump. "I was playing with my rock."

Considering the circumstances, the two shared a very long look.

The stalemate had stretched on long enough, the mutual shock was fading. The fae took a single look at what lay in front of him, and decided to make a judgement call.

"Evander, can you come here?"

His eyes travelled back to the troll.

"*Quickly.*"

Faster than sight, the vampire was among them—appearing so suddenly, it was like he'd manifested from the trees. Oddly enough, he didn't have any trouble spotting the troll.

No pesky rocks to distract him.

He took an involuntary step back, then froze very still.

"Is this a hazing?"

It was the last thing Kiera was expecting and the last thing for which Eden was prepared. He actually tore his eyes from the creature, giving the vampire a fleeting look.

"You overestimate my resources."

That was when the troll let out a roar.

Evander's face paled several degrees, but he stood his ground. One hand reached out, not for Kiera, but for the immortal standing between them. "Step away from it, please."

The troll's eyes flew from one to the other, like a falcon jumping between mice.

While none of them said it directly, each was struck with the feeling that if ever that gaze was allowed to settle...*that* person would not survive.

"I need to get Kiera."

Eden's voice was soft as nightingales, and strangely calm.

Her heart leapt, then faltered at the same time—squeezing out each pulse like the guilt was crushing it alive. She should not have called him. She should not have called any of them. It was her choice to wander away from camp. These were the consequences.

The vampire seemed to agree. At any rate, he did not value them the same.

He moved forward ever so slightly, like he was considering taking the fae by force. But whether he was wary of setting off the beast, or merely certain of the fae's inevitable reaction, he stayed where he was. Those fangs were glinting in the moonlight, pressing into his lip.

"What is the plan?" he asked softly, unable to hide the strain.

Eden was calm as ever, gazing up at the creature with the same eternal confidence as when he'd approached the frightened horse. "I'm going to change places, and throw her to you."

The creature bellowed again, eyes flashing between them.

"Change places?" Kiera echoed faintly, unable to even imagine such a thing, much less endorse it. "Eden, you can't—"

"No, that is a bad plan."

But as it turned out, the fae wasn't offering up his idea for discussion, so much as he was simply announcing it. He took a step forward, eyes on the troll, when Jesse burst through the trees.

Unlike the others, there was no delay in translation and no time lost to shock. The second he saw the beast, his mouth fell open and he reared back with a loud, "What the *hell*?!"

That was when several things happened.

The ground quaked below them. A flock of birds exploded from the trees. And a giant hand reached straight for Kiera, flying out of the darkness with an ungodly burst of speed.

But someone else reached her first.

"Take a breath."

There was a chance the fae was unaware of the image behind him. The monster's gaping jaw, the moonlight reflecting off its teeth. There was a chance he couldn't sense the hand flying towards him, already blowing the strands of his hair. There was a chance, though it certainly wasn't likely.

But it never showed on his face.

He caught her gaze for a suspended moment, radiating such irresistible calm, she found herself forgetting what was happening and thinking it might actually be okay. The night faded to a blur around them, the noise quieted to a hum, and his eyes twinkled with the very hint of a smile.

She took a breath.

He grabbed her a second later, catching her lightly around the waist and throwing her without hesitation towards Evander. The vampire caught her without looking, almost as an afterthought. His eyes were trained on Eden, wide and fixed with a look of silent dread.

She turned around just as the troll grabbed hold of him—those giant fingers closing into a fist where she'd been standing just moments before. There was a sudden exhale of breath, as all that weight clamped around his ribcage, then the fae vanished from sight.

He reappeared fifty feet in the air.

"EDEN!"

She and Jesse shouted at the same time, their voices blending together. There was suddenly a lot of shouting, but death didn't come for the fae just yet. Instead of lifting Eden immediately to its mouth, the creature took a moment to savor its prize—whipping him back and forth as though he weighed no more than a doll. If he'd been mortal, his neck would have already snapped.

As things stood...he was getting close.

"A little help!" he gasped.

Kiera clapped a hand over her mouth, staring in horror. "What can we do?!"

Evander picked up the fae's bow and fired two arrows, handling it with almost as much skill as the archer possessed himself. One of them glanced off the troll's brow, while the other grazed its eye. There was a mighty howl, and the creature's hand tightened around the fae's ribs.

"Not that!" Eden cried, struggling against those crushing fingers. There was little point. They had wrapped around him from knees to chest. "Anything but that!"

The friends shared a stricken glance, watching from what felt like miles away.

Jesse was already taking off his cloak, probably remembering a similar situation wherein he was the one held aloft by some monstrous creature and Eden sprinted up its leg. But even if he were to make the transformation, the others didn't see what good it would do. The odds of a single wolf making a difference against a cave troll were little better than if he happened to stay a man.

"Just think a moment," Kiera stammered, grabbing his sleeve to halt the process, "you can't tear him loose—we must get the creature to release him."

But they were out of time. And the troll was out of patience.

Without a hint of warning, it swung Eden towards its mouth—already looking towards the others, debating who would come next. It was the only bit of luck the fae received, because it didn't see when he ripped the silver clasp from his cloak and jammed it into the creature's gums.

It let out another earsplitting yowl as it jerked back in pain—swinging its arms in violent windmills and scraping the fae on the trees. There was a muffled cry, followed by a softer whimper.

A shower of blood hit the ground by their feet.

...seven hells.

Evander took a step forward, those immortal eyes blazing with rage.

He took an instant to consider his options, then he grabbed the sword from Jesse's belt and paced forward, burying it deep inside the beast's leg. It vanished to the hilt, but instead of ripping it out, he pushed it in still deeper—skewering through bone until it came through the other side.

The creature let out a hair-raising roar of fury. Its leg hobbled, bending slightly at the knee.

That was when he started climbing.

It was one of those moments that would remain lodged in Keira's brain forever, a visual that was impossible to truly forget. There was no pause between one movement and another, no time for panic let alone fear. Hands passed over hand, swinging lightly away from the forest floor, before the path was even and Evander merely paced forward, walking straight vertical up the side of the troll.

The vampire's logic was simple: if he couldn't get Eden down, he'd join him instead.

But there was nothing simple about what happened next.

"Seven hells…" Kiera breathed, taking a faltering step back.

She'd said it aloud this time, though there had scarcely been a moment that she and Jesse hadn't been thinking it. They were spectators now to games beyond what either could imagine, silent observers that could look but not touch, as the eternals above them passed into something more.

It didn't take long for Evander to scale the length of the troll, and the fae glanced up sharply the second he arrived. There was a moment when he stared in disbelieving silence, blinking slowly as strands of blood-matted hair fell into his eyes. Then his face tightened in misplaced concern.

"Evander?" he asked only to reaffirm it to himself, still unable to reconcile the sight of the vampire standing upon the monster's palm. "What are you—"

He choked into silence, coughing up a mouthful of blood.

The vampire was beside him in a moment, steadying the fae as best he could while discreetly testing the strength of those entrapping fingers at the same time. Whatever determination he made clearly wasn't to his liking. But he'd committed himself already; he was there to stay.

"It's a fine mess you've gotten yourself into," he murmured, kicking savagely at the troll's teeth as they were lifted again to its mouth. "Is this one of your habits? I'd like to be prepared."

The fae's eyes flashed with a trace of humor, followed by a thunderclap of pain. "Just go—"

"Right," Evander interrupted with a wry smile, dislodging a tooth and hurling it vengefully into the creature's eye. "I'm going to leave you up here alone. I think you know better than that."

Their eyes met for a brief moment. Then Eden looked away.

"What is your plan?" he asked softly.

The vampire took a moment to assess, then lifted slowly to his feet. His dark eyes caught those first searing rays of sunlight, as the endless night finally gave way to a new dawn.

"I'm going to take off that finger...and ram it down the beast's throat."

Somehow, even so far beneath the action, the words seemed to carry. Jesse and Kiera shared a stricken glance before jumping up and down, waving their arms and shouting at the same time.

The fae seemed to share the sentiment.

"No, that's...*that's* a bad plan," he stammered, echoing the vampire's earlier words.

"Oh no, are you worried?" Evander quipped, tilting his head to consider the angles as he prepared for the assault. "Does it freeze your chest with panic? Are you unable to pull in a breath? It might be good for you to worry about someone else for a change. It will at least be fair."

The fae stared in silence as he pushed to his feet—wedging the edge of his boot beneath the troll's yellowed claw. There was a faint splintering as he leveraged his strength against it. The second it was high enough, he took it in his arms, forcefully prying it away from the fae's body.

At that point, Kiera suddenly realized what was going to happen next.

"He's going to drop him," she gasped, reaching for Jesse. "Eden's about to fall."

No sooner had she said the words, than the troll's finger snapped backward, releasing the fae in the same instant. He plummeted in a free-fall towards the ground as the vampire spiraled in a tight circle, keeping a taut grip on his intended weapon and wrenching bone from bone.

Jesse caught hold of Eden just as the troll let out a high-pitched wail above them, throwing back its head and raging like a wounded bull. The vampire charged in the same moment, wielding the severed finger like a javelin and driving it straight into the creature's mouth.

"EVANDER!"

Eden's voice rang loud in the sudden quiet—echoing from tree to tree, as the vampire momentarily disappeared from sight. The troll made a sudden gagging motion, grabbing at its neck before its eyes abruptly widened and it let out an almost comical hiccup.

It crashed to the ground a second later, blood seeping into the earth.

The impact was so strong and the sound was so loud, that for a fleeting moment, the friends were able to register nothing further. The fae had fought his way from the shifter's arms, but the second his feet made contact with the ground, he toppled right back down, coughing in the dust.

It took a few seconds to settle. Then his eyes lifted to a pair of boots.

"Do you have any other fun ideas?" Evander asked crossly. "Or can we return to bed?"

Chapter 3

For the rest of the day, the fae wasn't precisely mobile.

With the utmost caution, the others checked to make sure the troll was no longer breathing, then made their way back to camp, only to find that the tent had collapsed when the ground started shaking. Jesse rebuilt it quickly and helped Eden inside—patiently ignoring the half-hearted protests as he removed the fae's shirt and wrapped a bandage carefully around his ribs. Most of them had been crushed in the monster's vice-like grip. Even an immortal would need a day to recover.

...they hoped.

"How is he?" Kiera asked quietly, the second the shifter stepped outside. It was hard to tell from the slew of profanities and threats that had echoed from inside. "I mean, he's clearly awake."

Jesse rubbed his eyes, flicking a piece of bloodied gauze from his cloak. "He's most definitely awake," he agreed wearily, "but apart from that, I could not tell you for certain. This isn't the first time he's been broken in a way that would kill a regular man. I never know where that line is for his people. I never know what's best for me to do."

Visit the seven hells, according to the fae. But it was a point well made. When dealing with immortal problems, it was often best to seek immortal advice.

"Should we go to the river again?" she asked softly. "Take him to see the naiads?"

Jesse gazed thoughtfully through the forest, as if he could see the sparkling water just beyond. "Yes, perhaps. Though we mustn't abuse such generosity. They might form a union."

The conversation stopped as the vampire walked back into camp.

Or we could ask someone who's seen this kind of injury before.

"Hello, Evander." Kiera greeted him sweetly, watching as he flung the wood he'd collected towards the fire with such unearthly force as to dent the surrounding rocks. "Have a nice walk?"

The vampire had not responded well to the incident with the troll.

It had started with the fae.

"Are you all right?" he'd asked quietly.

His voice was steady, but his eyes were wild with concern. When Eden had nodded weakly, then doubled over in pain, he'd knelt swiftly to the ground—uncoiling his body with gentle hands.

"It's all right," he soothed, brushing the fae's hair from his eyes, "the worst is over."

He propped him up delicately, unlacing the top of his shirt with a single hand. A pattern of violent bruises were already clouding up the base of his stomach, as though he'd spilled a jar of ink.

"There isn't much torn skin," he murmured, peeling back the tunic. "I doubt you'll need stitches. But some of these fractures might need to be set—"

He froze in surprise, as Eden pushed away his hand.

"It's all right," he panted, easing himself free. "Those are things I can do myself."

It was casually done, yet the rejection was unmistakable. The only question was whether his problem was with the vampire touching his bare skin, or the copious amounts of blood. The others froze across the trampled clearing while Evander jerked back his arm like he'd been given a burn.

"We have asked so much of you already, there is no need to add to the burden," Eden added quickly, though he kept his eyes safe on the ground. "Thank you, Evander. I am in your debt."

The trouble had continued with the troll.

"It's definitely dead," Jesse said as confirmation, though after witnessing its final moments, no one had doubted the alternative. He nudged it with his shoe, then paused suddenly, looking the body up and down. A second later, his eyes lifted to the vampire. "Do you want to...maybe...?"

Evander glanced across the clearing, rigid as a stone. "What?"

The shifter blushed furiously, already regretting bringing it up. "There's a lot of blood. Might last you for a while."

Without knowing the exact reason, Kiera was suddenly certain this was a rather terrible thing to say. The vampire's jaw tightened, and for a split second, that newfound patience waned.

"I would not drink such a thing, any more than you would eat it." He glanced down at the fae before pacing abruptly in the opposite direction. "We are not the savages you might think."

At that point, Jesse had wisely extracted Eden from the clearing.

It wasn't until they were limping away that Kiera saw the grooves in the earth and realized how fast the vampire must have changed directions to reach him. It wasn't until she saw the cracks in the stone that she realized it almost wasn't fast enough. He almost hadn't gotten there in time.

"We almost lost him."

She said it quietly, almost to herself. But Evander froze dead still beside her. His lovely face tightened with a look that was impossible to describe before settling on something rather cold.

"It's only a matter of time," he replied shortly. "We should prepare for that now."

From the looks of things, that sentiment had not improved.

"Would you like to see him?" she asked softly, gesturing with a tilt of her head.

Instead of standing guard at the entrance of the tent like she might have expected, Evander had kept a marked distance from the fae, as if he could no longer stand the sight. When she had casually inquired as to the reason, the vampire replied that he was *giving the fae time to grow a brain.*

"I think he'd like to see you," she coaxed gently. "I think he'd like to say thanks."

Evander spared her the barest of glances before turning away. "He said it already. There is no need to say it again."

She stared a moment longer, then let out a quiet sigh. The immortals matched each other in every other regard. It should have come as no surprise that they also matched each other in pride.

"Alright, well—"

"I am going hunting," he interrupted tersely. "I will be back before dawn."

He was gone before the others had time to register the statement, before they could even see in which direction he'd gone. Jesse glanced around the empty trees, as if there might still be a chance to catch him, before letting out a tired sigh of his own.

"I guess I'll be keeping watch then," he muttered, settling by the fire. "*All* night..."

Kiera stood a moment longer, then slipped inside the tent.

Eden was propped up exactly where Jesse had left him, angled like a broken king atop all their earthly belongings in the vague hope that the bones in his chest would someone manage to set.

He glanced up immediately as she entered. Beautiful as ever, but white as a ghost. "Where is the vampire?"

She paused in the entryway, wondering if he realized how many times he'd asked that precise question since Evander had burst into their lives.

"He's not here," she answered evasively, not wanting to make him feel any worse. "I think he was going to...to fetch some water for the flasks."

Eden absorbed this without blinking, never breaking her gaze. "He doesn't wish to see me?"

You cannot lie to a fae.

She didn't even attempt it. She changed the subject instead.

"Why did you tell me to breathe?" she asked abruptly. "In that moment when you appeared in front of me...it was the only thing you said. Not to run, not to duck. Just to breathe."

He gazed up at her, having already forgotten the moment himself. "I was about to throw you a long distance and very hard. If there wasn't something to bolster your ribs when you landed, there was a chance they might break."

She nodded with a belated shiver, trying to act more composed than she felt.

"Did *you* take a breath? Before Jesse caught you?"

He tried to smile, but it was more of a grimace. "...not so much." He shifted aside to make room, as she settled on the blankets beside him, adding a lighthearted, "It's always easier to remember these things for other people."

She nodded slowly, then slapped him across the face. "You enjoyed that."

His hair flew back and he sucked in a quick breath—staring back at her with a mixture of pain and surprise. Outside the tent, Jesse glanced up sharply as well—debating whether he wanted to go inside, before deciding that he was much happier tending to the fire.

"I enjoyed that?" he repeated, once he'd gathered the breath to speak. He lifted a reflexive hand, then lowered it just as fast—purposely ignoring the angry welt rising on his face.

"Not this," she gestured to the bed, then pointed back to the woods, "back there."

His eyes flashed with temper, but he spoke with a perfect calm. "You called for *me*," he answered flatly. "I was in a completely different part of the forest, keeping watch, when you somehow walked into a troll. I saved your life—"

"—and you loved every second," she finished, shaking her head. "This whole thing, this whole *terrible* plan...it couldn't have worked out any better for you. Since we left Farion, you've been searching for a reason not to return. Since we left the hollow, you can't even hide your smile."

He lowered his gaze, twisting his fingers in the blanket. "I've been trying to lift spirits."

"We are likely marching to our death," she said flatly. "This isn't the time to lift spirits and take stupid chances. This is the time to make plans. I did not wish for this outcome. Neither did Jesse, neither did Evander. We do not want to face down a dragon by ourselves."

"We are not facing down anything—"

He fell silent at the look on her face.

There was no point in denying it. From the moment the idea entered his head, the fae had been utterly consumed. He parted his lips to reply, then bowed his head to his chest.

"I do not mean to twist your arm. Regardless of personal sentiment, everything I said at the hollow was true. If this is the situation...there *isn't* another way. This is the only—"

"This is exactly what you want. Another monster, another adventure. Another way to avoid whatever things you're running from, that make it so bloody easy for you to upend our lives."

A cold silence fell between them. One that told her she'd gone too far.

It was difficult to chastise a man in such a condition, especially given that nothing he'd said was technically untrue. It made sense, the points he'd made about the dragon. And he'd just thrown his body in front of a cave troll in a desperate gamble to save her life.

But nothing I said was untrue either.

He pulled in a breath, searching for patience. "You are upset—"

"I'm right." She got up and walked to the door. Then she let out a sigh. "Eden...I'm upset."

She glanced over her shoulder, expecting to see him still angry. But there wasn't a hint of frustration on that lovely face. If anything, the fae looked uncharacteristically repentant.

"I cannot blame you for that," he said softly. "There is truth in everything you said. And whatever hand we have been given, this is much to put on one so young."

The face of another immortal burned through her mind.

"It is much to put on anyone," she answered. "Especially those who are doomed to care."

THE VAMPIRE CAME BACK much sooner than any of them had expected, meaning Jesse would no longer have to keep watch for the four of the after the sun went down. It was already starting to slip behind the trees when Eden wandered out of the tent and found them by the fire. His shirt was gone, but a blanket was wrapped around his shoulders. He shivered a little in the breeze.

"Is everything all right?" Jesse asked swiftly, half-pushing from his seat. "I could try to find some more of that—"

Eden shook his head quickly, glancing at the vampire. "May I speak with you?"

"You should get some rest," Evander answered without looking up from the flames. "Gods know what trouble you'll find in the morning."

There was a moment of silence, followed by a quiet sigh.

"...please?"

Evander's eyes lifted, staring with a fixed gaze at the forest. Then he pushed abruptly to his feet and crossed the campsite, looking with the same expressionless gaze at the fae. "Speak then."

Eden's eyes flickered to the others, and his hand tightened upon the blanket. There wasn't a great chance he'd make it very far in the forest, but he was certainly willing to try. "Perhaps somewhere with a little—"

"Right here is fine."

In hindsight, the vampire might have regretted insisting on that point.

Eden stared at him for a long time, almost as if he was searching for the words on Evander's own face. A rush of emotion heated his skin before leaving a kind of hollow in its wake.

"I'm sorry," he murmured, almost too soft for the mortals to hear. "Every time I hear you sigh, every time your brow tightens...I'm sorry, Evander. I never wish you cause you any pain."

The vampire was frozen so unnaturally still, Kiera might have thought he'd been turned to stone. She couldn't see the look on his face, only the dark ripples of his hair, but it must have been something truly extraordinary, because the fae proceeded with the greatest of care.

"When you first began travelling with us," he continued quietly, "when I asked why you had spared me—you said that you didn't know. You asked if *I* knew the reason." He paused a moment, then shook his head. "I still do not. You are an enigma to me, Evander. A perplexity I have never before seen. I do not always understand you. I do not believe you always understand me. But if you are certain of nothing else, please let it be this...I never wish to do *anything* that might hurt you."

If only he'd been able to leave it there. If only there was a less difficult road that lay between them. But he added one final conclusion, something between a whisper and a thought.

"There are some things I cannot give you."

Chapter 4

Jesse took the first watch. Evander took the second. So when Kiera opened her eyes the next morning, all three of the friends were pressed against each other inside the tent.

It was a crunch they hadn't known before the addition of the vampire. It would never have been possible, because one of them would always have been on watch. And despite emerging each morning in a state of mild asphyxiation, it was hard not to feel rather tender about it as well.

Keira turned ever so slightly, warming with a restful smile.

Her boys.

She'd never admit it aloud, but that was the way she'd started to think about them. Not the most accurate description, given that one of them had been roaming under the stars for centuries, but when they slept, all of those timelines vanished. Their differences and stories blended into a shared adolescence, and the muted light painted them all the same. It had been in precisely such a moment, the moniker first popped into her head. She'd been using it in secret every day since.

That morning, they didn't disappoint.

They had each adjusted to each other's habits—in that they bore them now with relatively little complaint—but the result had made each one slightly peculiar themselves. Jesse had a tendency to steal the others' blankets, so Eden's hand stayed curled around the edge of his even in sleep. The fae often took a moment to fully orient upon waking, and spoke those first greetings in his native tongue, rather than their own. And each of the men had begun to openly hate Kiera's long hair.

It was a net, Eden had once described it. *A suffocating, vindictive net.*

It was perhaps the greatest contradiction of all. Despite their apocalyptic circumstance, they gathered together at the end of each day. Just three teenagers caught on a never-ending camping trip.

The three least likely teenagers to have ever met.

She squirmed beneath the blankets a little, feeling two sets of legs pressing into her on either side. The first few times they'd attempted such a sleeping arrangement, Jesse had subtly positioned himself to be always between the barmaid and the fae. But they had reached such a level of trust, he no longer seemed to mind. It was Kiera who minded now, always trapped like a child in the middle.

I have lost all feeling in my legs.

She tried and failed to wiggle her toes.

Those bastards.

On that cheery note, she propped onto her elbows and prepared to announce her plight to the others, only to find that Eden was already awake. You'd never have known by a mere glance at him. She'd never met a person who could freeze so completely still. But those blue eyes were open.

They had been open for a long time.

"Morning," she said softly.

He startled and glanced in her direction—staring blankly for a moment, before his eyes dilated into focus. "Sorry, what did you say?"

There was something so disarmingly childlike about him in those moments, she could never find it in her heart to tease him. It was even more endearing when he forgot himself and spoke fae.

"Never mind."

Jesse's breathing hitched and he stirred beside her—reaching blindly for the girl he'd been cuddling with, only to find himself squeezing Eden's hand by mistake.

The fae glanced down with a hint of surprise before lifting his eyes with a wry grin. "Good morning, sweetheart."

Jesse pressed his face into the pillow with a groan. "We should have gotten a bigger tent."

"No, this could be an interesting new dynamic," the fae answered mischievously, refusing to release him. "Just imagine the possibilities. I could get you to carry books for me as well."

Jesse yanked at his wrist, and Eden released him immediately—feeling the slightest of tears, as his arm was stretched further than he'd planned. Kiera only saw the wince because she was still pressed against him. It was how she got a closer look at his ribcage as well.

"Look at you..."

Evander had said there wasn't much torn skin, but there was clearly a bit. The bandage Jesse had wrapped around his chest was already stained through. But that wasn't the worst part. The worst part was the bruises, not even the violent color, but the symmetry. Line after line, finger stacked atop finger. The troll might have died in the forest, but his legacy was imprinted in the fae's skin.

Eden fidgeted uncomfortably under her gaze. "Kiera, I was only teasing about the—"

"You know what I forgot to say the other night?" she interrupted quietly, still staring at the bandage. "Probably the most important thing, but it completely slipped my mind."

His eyes flashed up warily, resting on her face. "I couldn't imagine. You said a lot."

She sat there a moment longer, then met his gaze. "Thank you."

The tension vanished, as those blades they so seldom used against each other, lowered back to their sides. His face softened immediately, and he flicked her cheek with the trace of a smile.

"You're welcome."

The two locked eyes, and a silent reconciliation was made.

"But we have greater problems now," he continued abruptly, that enchanting face growing stern. "Like how exactly you managed to *walk into a cave troll* in the first place."

She closed her eyes with a pained expression, as Jesse picked up on the trail.

"That's a question I've been asking myself..."

He proceeded to embark upon a lecture that would have made his friends proud, if either had been paying attention. But Kiera had learned to tune such things out long before, and she was struck with the sudden suspicion that the fae might have been casting attention away from himself.

He'd slipped away the moment the shifter started talking, dressing in silence and throwing occasional glances at the door—like he was afraid of what might be waiting on the other side.

Or what might not be waiting.

"I'm sure he's still here," she whispered comfortingly.

Eden lifted another finger to his ear, but rolled his eyes with an exasperated grin.

The shifter eventually ranted himself out. They dug around in packs, folded their blankets, and forced their feet into boots that had yet to dry from the previous day's rain. The instant all three of them were ready, the fae pulled back the door—only to pause immediately in the frame.

Evander was sitting beside the fire, a beaming smile upon his face.

If they actually were the world's unlikeliest of teenagers, the vampire was the one who'd been left out the most often in the rain. *Literally.* There was a fading imprint in the leaves where he'd lain down to rest and a sprinkling of dew in his raven hair. It caught the light when he paced towards them, flinging into the air like a hailstorm of little diamonds raining to the ground.

"You're still here," Eden blurted without thinking.

Over the duration of the nighttime hours, he'd come up with several things to say, whether the vampire had remained or not. None had been so simple. None had been so blunt.

Evander's eyes twinkled with a smile.

"Where else would I go?" he teased. "I told you already, I've committed myself to stay."

The others shared a quick look behind Eden's back before discreetly extracting themselves from the conversation and settling beside the fire. Much as they liked to pry, there was something troublesome about doing it in such close proximity. They would do it from a distance instead.

Eden lingered uncertainly by the tent. Evander lingered in front of him.

While he was usually the one averting his gaze and making conversational exits, the vampire seemed cheerfully determined that morning to stand his ground and force the fae to speak his mind.

"You seem...well."

Kiera grimaced sympathetically as the fae unraveled before her very eyes. All of the quick deflections and clever jabs he'd been practicing turned to ash beneath the vampire's steady gaze.

Evander nodded slowly, still smiling. "I am well."

There was a creak in the logs around the fire as Jesse leaned discreetly closer—whispering in Kiera's ear. "This is *riveting*. You should add it to that poem."

For possibly the first time ever, neither of the immortals seemed to hear them. They were in their own world, playing by a set of rules that only one of them seemed to fully understand.

Eden regarded him cautiously, like there was something beneath that smile to fear.

"The other night," he began softly, "I was not speaking lightly—"

"I understood what you were saying." Evander's eyes twinkled as they looked him up and down, lingering on the blood-stained clothes and interseting bruises. "And you have made it easy. You are far less compelling this way."

For the second time, the fae was merely stunned. He stood there straight-backed and lost as a misfired arrow, searching desperately for words that would never come. By the time he came back to his senses, the vampire had already left and joined Jesse by the fire. A piece of parchment had been smoothed onto a stone between them, covered in etchings and tiny scribbles of ink.

Kiera leaned forward curiously, examining it for the first time.

"Is this a map?" she asked in surprise. "Where did you get it?"

"We didn't get it," Jesse answered with a touch of pride, "we made it last night—me and Evander. Well, *mostly* Evander. But he's been wandering the realm for a very long time."

She looked between them, shocked to the core.

To be honest, she didn't know what was more surprising. That the vampire and the shifter had willingly embarked upon a group-activity, or that one had allowed the other to take credit.

In the end, she settled on the most insignificant of questions.

"...how did you get the parchment?"

There was a brief pause, then Jesse cleared his throat. "We tore a page from the back of your book."

She lifted her head slowly, leveling them with the same murderous look. A sudden hush fell over the clearing as they stared back in silence. Jesse was apologetic. Evander was blank.

"There was nothing on it," he said flatly.

The shifter dropped his eyes to the ground, trying to keep from smiling.

"*Proceed.*"

"Right, well...this is a rendering of the realm as best as Evander remembers it." Jesse knelt to the ground beside it, eager to continue with the presentation. "There are apparently several places that get hot enough to be appealing to a dragon, but most of them are at least sparsely populated."

Eden wandered over with a frown as she glanced in confusion between them.

"Why would that be a problem?" she asked. "What does a dragon mind if a place happens to be populated? You'd think they would prefer it."

"But it would have been spotted," Evander interjected quietly. "In my experience, dragons do not kill neatly. There would have been survivors, and they would have spread the word."

Kiera looked up slowly, fixing on his face. "...in your experience?"

The vampire shrugged, as if such things could scarcely be avoided.

"I have seen a dragon," he admitted. "From a distance, long ago, and not the kind that you have described. It would likely have been much smaller. And still, the wingspan was immense." His face stilled at the memory before he forced himself onward. "At any rate, most creatures will not make a nest somewhere it can be disturbed. If we are searching for a land both hot and isolated..."

He pointed to a far-flung spot on the map.

"That is the only place which comes to mind."

Like they'd planned it, the rest of them leaned closer—peering down at the map.

To be honest, the rolling valleys and jagged peaks made little sense to Kiera. Yes, she could understand what they represented, but each one was layered atop another and there were too many to keep track. While the others saw past the topography to things like population centers and the fastest path through an agricultural sprawl, she was blown away by the sheer scale. She could have stood there looking for hours, poring over every inch of it. A place she'd lived her entire life.

"What do you think?" Jesse asked quietly, studying Eden's face for a reaction. It had felt strange making plans with the vampire as he slept. "I mean, we need to head somewhere..."

The fae nodded slowly, never taking his eyes from the map.

Since leaving the Marrow's house, the companions had been travelling *west* with no particular destination, just as they'd been travelling *north* in the weeks before. There was a strange comfort in it, like if they

went far enough, they might simply see a dragon in the clouds and follow it home.

"I have never been that far across the sea myself," he admitted, staring at the map with a thoughtful frown. "I know of no one who has.
Perhaps one man. But we can no longer ask him."

Several times, his eyes flickered back towards the mainland, towards places he was familiar with himself. There were deserts there as
well, endless scorching plains. But the vampire was right about the people. If a three-headed dragon was torching the skies, they would have
heard.

"It is a good rendering," he remarked, almost without thinking. "It
makes me wonder how you know some of these places so well."

Evander hesitated, then smiled. "You need only ask me."

The two shared a swift glance.

"It is a remarkable rendering," Kiera murmured, winding her fingers along an intricately drawn river. "But why must you lay it all out
like this? If we'll all be staying together...?"

Before she even finished the sentence, she understood her mistake.
Her cheeks flushed with embarrassment, but in case there was any confusion, Jesse tapped his finger upon the edge.

"You need to memorize it," he said quietly. "We all need to memorize it. In case something should happen...this quest is too important to
fail because not all of us knew the route."

To her great surprise, it was Evander who took her through it.

Together, the two of them followed his musical voice up through
the Seraphine Forest, and down again through the river country—where the people were hearty, and the earth sucked the boots
from your legs. Up again to the frosted mountains—avoiding for some
reason, the wide valley in the middle—before pouring out near a dwar-
ven settlement at the base of the wooded peaks. A hundred tiny land-
marks stood out along the way, but those were the points they were

looking for. If they managed to make it through all that, there was just the small matter of crossing the Great Sea.

The vampire did not usually speak so much. She got the feeling he was making a concerted effort to try. Whatever the reason, he was a patient teacher. He'd ask her questions, point out details that she hadn't thought of—imprinting the image slowly into her mind, so that in the end, she did not need to scramble for answers. It was more like remembering a picture.

She sat there a long time after he was gone. Remembering with a smile.

THERE WERE SOME DAYS when the hike set before the friends seemed endless. The scenery, while beautiful, held no variation, and every league that passed beneath their feet blended into the next. It was not that way for the next week that they travelled. It was like wandering in a dream.

"What about those ones?" Kiera asked excitedly, pointing to a cluster of crystallite flowers on the side of the trail. "Eden, what are those ones called?"

He let out a patient sigh. "Those are imoneth."

She bounded past him, forgetting the rules that forbade her from ever walking first upon the forest trail. "And those? What about those?"

"They are haydocin."

She stared as long as her attention would allow, marveling at the delicate iridescence, before spring-boarding to the next. A grove of silver-tipped roses. Sprigs of cantiss and larkspurs of the clearest blue. She tripped over a tangle of what looked like sackerlilies before catching herself on the trailing branches of the trees above them, each one tipped with blossoms of a vivid tangerine.

"What about these?" she breathed, trailing her fingers through them. "Eden?"

He glanced over with a hint of irritation. The usual indulgence was long ago spent. "Kiera, I've told you already. You're not even trying to remember—"

She appeared in front of him, red-cheeked and grinning ear to ear. "This is impossibly lovely. I think we should stay."

He stared for a split second before breaking with a quiet laugh. A pair of light fingers tucked back her hair, and without seeming to think about it, he pressed a sudden kiss to her forehead. "Perhaps you will come back to this place," he remarked, as they continued strolling along the trail. "It's unlikely the dragon will eat *all* of us...perhaps this is where you wish to remain."

In truth, it was a question she had deliberately refrained from asking herself. The task set before them had swollen to take up all available space. She could not imagine anything after.

"Perhaps this is where you wish to remain as well," she replied with a little grin.

While he'd been making an observation, she'd been making a joke. The fae would not *remain* anywhere. Such stagnancy wasn't in his blood. That being said, he was clearly in his element.

There was something about such natural beauty that made him light up from the inside. The bruises from the troll were fading, each breath was a little easier than the one before. When the wind picked up and the air scented with the blooms above them, she could almost see the color returning to his face, like a man coming back to life.

As usual, she was not the only one to have noticed. The brighter the fae shone, the more the vampire seemed to warm around him—drifting on the periphery before venturing close as he dared.

He ghosted up behind him, falling in pace alongside.

"Would you like me to eat the girl?"

Her heart faltered, and she slipped upon the trail.

"That's a bold joke, vampire." Eden threw him a sharp look, though he couldn't help but smile. It was the same joke he'd made many times himself. "Though it's not entirely unwarranted."

Jesse shoved past them, draping an arm across her shoulders. "Eden, if you encourage this, I will strangle you with those bloomin' braids."

The fae chuckled softly, watching as they stormed up ahead.

"I like your braids," Evander murmured, catching one with a flick of his hand and trailing it through his fingers. "I've always wondered how they might feel."

Eden froze where he stood, right in the middle of the trail.

His body was still, but his heart was pounding, as if he'd run a great ways and then come to a sudden stop. Although he did not pull away himself, there was such a look on his face that Evander lowered his hand slowly, looking almost nervous to have found himself so close.

The fae's eyes lifted then, burning like a brand.

Do not touch.

He didn't say it aloud. He didn't have to. It scorched the air between them, like the thrill of lightning before a storm. Before Evander could say a word, he knocked past him—sweeping past the others and vanishing up the trail. The rest of them stood in awkward silence before heading silently after him. In a move that was perhaps unwise, Kiera slackened her pace to match Evander's.

"I know what you wish," she said quietly, "this is not the way to do it."

It was a tricky thing, offering advice to a person who'd been alive for hundreds of years. It was trickier still, when that person happened to be a vampire. But despite the obvious differences between them, she couldn't help but feel the slightest bit protective of Evander. Perhaps it was the natural reaction to seeing someone wishing so earnestly, being shot down every time.

It was why she was so surprised by the vampire's smile.

"You are sweet," he remarked without inflection, like he was noticing for the first time. "But in this case, we disagree. Think on your own troubles, darling." He winked. "I will think on mine."

He swept up the trail without another word, leaving she and Jesse frozen in his wake. They stared after him for a moment before turning back to each other.

"Did he just call you darling?" the shifter asked in astonishment.

Did he just wink?

She shook her head slowly, setting off once again. "The world is upside-down."

IN WHAT WOULD LATER be described as an act of betrayal, Jesse volunteered to go hunting that evening. He also volunteered Kiera to go with him.

"Must I?" she complained, dragging her shoes in the dirt.

It wasn't that she was particularly squeamish, the girl had spent the last few years dutifully decapitating fish. But there was something different about being there when it actually happened, bearing witness to the moment the light vanished from a creature's eyes.

"Come on, it will be fun." Jesse took her wrist with a grin and dragged her casually into the trees, muttering under his breath. "A lot more fun than sticking around here."

Things had not gotten easier between the fae and the vampire. If anything, those tensions were poised to break. There had been not a word between them since that fateful moment. When Evander made a casual comment about the weather, Eden started playing with a blade.

"If you think the shared pleasure of a ritualistic killing is a 'fun' way for couples to bond, then we have more serious problems than I thought." She marched petulantly through the dense underbrush, swatting manically at the air. "Did you see the size of that bug?"

Jesse smiled to himself, then glanced over his shoulder. "You called us a couple."

Her heart stilled. "...would you not?"

"I would."

The two shared a secret smile.

"But you should know that I've been seeing other people," he continued apologetically.

She let out a breath of laughter, sliding her hand into his. "Cheating already? Wow."

He nodded to himself as they walked along, holding back branches to let her through. "There was this goblin at the last tavern we visited. And a starlit crone in the woods before that. She asked me to make something of my life, and I left her." He shook his head sadly, like the memory still weighed heavy on his mind. "I've regretted it every day since."

Kiera laughed again, scaring away any potential animals they were supposed to find. It was a fact she remembered a second later, shooting a reflexive glance back towards the camp.

"I'm afraid we're fated to be the only couple."

Jesse scoffed, as if he'd seen worse. "I'm not so sure about that."

She stopped walked, laughing again. "You *can't* be serious. I thought Eden was going to cut off his fingers and reenact that grisly scene with the troll."

Jesse smiled as well, remembering that quick flash of the blade. "I'm not saying anything's going to happen...but you can tell they like each other."

"Oh yeah?" she quipped. "How?"

"Because they watch each other."

There was something so simple about the way he said it, borderline naïve, though she sensed a deeper wisdom at the same time. Perhaps it *was* that simple. Perhaps the rest was just foolishness of their own making. Perhaps it was not so uncommon, but plagued every couple just the same.

"Easy as that, huh?"

He shrugged, blushing with a shy smile. "...I watch you."

DINNER WAS A STRAINED affair that night, and equally brief. The moment the rest of them were finished eating, Eden kicked some dirt over the fire, and set about cleaning up the meal.

"I will meet you inside," he said without looking, as the others filed into the tent.

He had been rushing things along the entire evening, like he was fearful to allow too much silence to pass. With a lot less care than usual, he dumped out the remains of their meal and began scrubbing vigorously at the fire-licked caldron—whitened knuckles clutched upon a rag.

He didn't see the vampire come up beside him. Not until he was sliding it from his hands.

"Can I help you with this?"

Eden froze beneath his touch, taking a breath to steady himself. A terrible silence stretched on between them before he raised his head slowly, staring deep into the vampire's eyes. *"Stop."*

The pot was forgotten as the two men lifted slowly to their feet.

"I was going to stop," Evander said quietly, standing his ground. "After the other night, I truly was." He warmed with that same inexplicable smile. "But then you told me not to."

"Are you addled?" Eden said sharply, fighting the urge to smack him upside the head. "That is *not* what I said, vampire."

"But it's what I heard, angel." Evander flicked him beneath the chin, pairing it with the world's most infuriating wink. "Try to keep up."

He left the fae standing beside the fire, trembling with such bottled fury, it was a miracle it didn't explode right out of him. It wasn't until he turned slowly around, still rigid as a blade, that Kiera and Jesse had the sense to scramble away from the door of the tent.

It flew open a second later, letting in a gust of cold air.

"I think I may kill him."

With most people, such a thing could be written off as mere exaggeration. But the fae were not generally prone to exaggeration, and Eden looked like death itself.

Kiera lifted her hands, trying to appear rational. "I think you may wish to sleep on that. It seems a shame to travel so far with someone, only to end up killing them before the end."

"It isn't a shame," Eden replied, still frozen by the entry. "It happens every day."

The quiet chorus of laughter from outside unspooled him still further.

"Take off your boots, Jesse. I will need you to shift." He held out a blind hand, firing off orders like a wartime general. "And give me that blade."

Jesse shook his head, backing carefully out of reach. "I was asked to show leniency with the vampire." He flashed a winning smile. "This is me being lenient."

At that point, since it was already going to be a terrible night, Kiera decided she might as well make it even worse. "I don't suppose you've given any thought to—"

"He is most certainly NOT sleeping inside the tent!"

Chapter 5

"*Happy birthday to you...*"

Kiera awoke the next morning to a gentle kiss, not unlike the one she'd been dreaming about just a few seconds before. The only difference was that when she opened her eyes, there were two men sitting on the bed, instead of just one. They smiled at the same time, then Eden leaned closer.

"Now guess which of us that was."

Jesse shoved him with a grin while she pushed drowsily onto her elbows—the familiar sing-song still ringing in her ears. The world blinked quickly into focus, but she still couldn't string things together. She simply stared in sleepy confusion, half-hidden behind tangles of hair.

"How did you know it was my birthday?" she asked in astonishment.

Jesse squeezed her ankle beneath the covers, those green eyes twinkling as they swept her up and down. "It was one of the first things you told me, in the woods before we reached Farion. You said you were born on the last day of spring."

...I did?

Those early days felt so long ago, she could scarcely remember. And she had apparently been the one talking. If she could scarcely remember, then how in the world did he?

"And that's today?" She hitched herself up with a hint of embarrassment. A girl should know her eighteenth birthday. "How did you possibly...?" She trailed off, looking at the fae.

"My people are rather attune to those things," he said with a teasing smile. "We wouldn't be very good custodians of this place otherwise." He leaned back on his heels. "I cannot remember the mortal consensus, but are you of age now? Is this when you're said to have left childhood behind?"

A typical immortal question, to a typical mortal affair.

"I have always been *of age*, thank you very much." She tossed back her hair with a dainty scowl, but by now, she was grinning like all the rest. "I've always been a great deal more mature than you."

Eden nodded slowly before lighting with sudden mischief. "I may now attempt to court you." He turned in preemptive triumph to the shifter. "Are you worried?"

Jesse shot him a sideways look. "I don't know how you could attempt to court anyone with those repellant ears."

She threw open her arms. "Do not quarrel—it is my birthday! Let us go to the carnival! Let us go dancing in the city square! Let us treat each other to a fine dinner, followed by a relaxing soak in the tub!"

The men smiled sympathetically. Their muddy boots were in a line by the door.

"I'll tell you what," Jesse began cautiously, hedging his bets, "how about *instead* of doing that...we walk to the hottest place on earth to do battle with a dragon?"

There was a scathing silence, then she pushed past him out of the tent.

"I cannot believe you would make that joke on my birthday."

Eden lingered a moment longer before shaking his head. "I cannot believe you would make that joke on her birthday."

KIERA TOOK A STEP OUTSIDE the tent, blinking in the bright sunlight, then froze like an arrow had pinned her to the ground. The camp was there as she'd left it, except it was nothing like how she'd left it. A spare blanket had been set in the grass in the middle, laden with a woodland feast.

It was all of her favorites.

There were bursts of wisteria and snowbells dripped in honey. Huckleberries and walnuts, with a handful of patiently shelled pistachios on the side. Freshly picked apples, still warm from the morning sun, had been set beside a pitcher of water with tiny lavender petals still floating inside.

Not a rodent in sight.

"You did this?"

Eden swept past her without answering, but Jesse paused by her side. His arm found its way, as it so often did, to her shoulders and they regarded the blanket together.

"Not just me, Eden insisted upon helping. Then he insisted upon taking charge." He slipped into a hilarious impression. "We must make a great fuss. She would love a great fuss."

She let out a breath of laughter, leaning against him with a giant grin.

He was right!

The last birthday she'd celebrated had been before her shift at the tavern. A quick bite of pastry from the baker's before back to scrubbing pitchers and descaling the day's fish.

She suspected this year would be much better.

"Such commotion for a mortal's birthday." Evander swept into the clearing, his dark eyes twinkling with a smile. "All so we can celebrate her decaying before our very eyes."

"Come now," Eden chided, "they don't get many of those."

In honor of the occasion, it appeared the immortals had called a temporary truce. One was standing a great distance from the other, but it was a truce nonetheless.

Kiera clapped her hands in delight and hurried to examine the table—explaining with great authority the significance of each item as Jesse indulged her with a grin. The men stared after her with the same smile before their eyes slowly drifted to each other. In another contrast from the day before, Eden's hair fell loose to his shoulders, pulled half-back in the custom of his people.

Not a braid in sight.

"Evander—"

"I'm sorry," the vampire interrupted quietly. His gaze never faltered, but his voice was sincere. "I did not wish to upset you." He paused. "I will not ask to help with the washing again."

Eden stared back without a hint of emotion, regarding him in silence. Then all at once, a trace of humor warmed the edges of his face. "It's for the best. You would have been terrible at it."

They turned away from each other, both harboring secret smiles.

"So tell us, princess..." Jesse leaned forward on his elbows as the others settled around the blanket, whether they had any intention of eating or not. There was a stain of berries around his lips, yet his eyes narrowed shrewdly as a teacher on examination day. "How do you feel?"

By now, Kiera had fashioned herself a crown of mayflowers, and had silently vowed not to remove it until her *next* birthday. She considered a weighted moment, then offered a grave reply.

"*Entirely* different." She threw a disdainful glance at the immortals, as if the act of explaining would be quite tiresome. "You wouldn't understand."

Eden laughed aloud, even Evander had to smile.

It had been said as a jest, but she realized all at once how truly strange it must have been for them. To give such prominence to a single day, to celebrate with someone at the dawn of such an inevitably short life. Did they even celebrate birthdays anymore? Or was that a mortal consolation?

"I have no gift for you," Eden said apologetically, gesturing vaguely to the woods, "options were in limited supply. But I wrote an inscription in one of your books." When she pushed at once to retrieve it, he caught her sleeve. "I would ask that you keep it to yourself."

Quite mysterious.

"Alright..."

The two shared a hidden smile.

"I have something for you as well," Evander said unexpectedly, reaching beneath the blanket and pulling up a bouquet of the same crystallite flowers she'd been marveling at before.

"These were half a day's journey behind us," she said in surprise, still dazzled by the sight of them. "Over six leagues across the slopes—"

"And now they are here. For your birthday."

Detached as the vampire could be, there was something remarkably observant about him as well. He noticed little things about the rest of them, other might have missed. Things they avoided, things that made them smile. It might have seemed trivial, but vampires were not used to smiles. He was learning to horde them, seeking them out wherever he could.

Sometimes, a bit more pointedly than others.

"You may enjoy them," he added, nudging them closer in a silent command.

She picked up the bouquet, deliberately avoiding the eyes of the others, then lifted it to her face for a fragrant sniff. Like silver and sunlight. And something else, cloyingly sweet.

"They're lovely." She beamed at him. "Thank you, Evander."

He walked away with a little smile of his own, feeling pleased. It wasn't until he'd vanished into the woods and she lifted them again, that Eden reached over and caught her wrist.

"Those are poison."

She turned to him incredulously.

"...what?"

"They are sleepers," he confided softly, "toxic in large quantities, though we sometimes use small bits in our ointments and salves. To Evander's credit, I don't think he knew."

Why would he? What use does a vampire have for such knowledge?

"Do not lick your fingers," Jesse whispered teasingly. "You'll miss the rest of the day."

She gave them a bracing look, then threw them as far as she could into the forest—towards the ravine, where the vampire would not see them by mistake. She washed her hands carefully when she was finished, trickling them with lavender water and wiping them on the blanket.

It was not a spare blanket, she realized. It was Evander's.

Her head lifted suddenly at the thought.

"That was incredibly thoughtful," she murmured quietly, staring at the place where he'd wandered into the trees. "I would never have guessed him thoughtful when he first arrived."

Eden flashed her a look, but said nothing.

"You can't be talking about Evander," Jesse exclaimed, laughing at the thought. "Our resident vampire—that's the thoughtful creature of whom you speak?"

She elbowed him in the ribs, so hard the crown slipped into her eyes. "I thought you were coming round to him," she accused, pushing it back to center.

"As a cartographer—yes. As a boon companion—that is a resounding *no*." Jesse chuckled again, shaking his head. "The man leaves no footprints. He doesn't even smile—"

"He smiles," Eden interrupted, lifting his head. For a moment those eyes, which could be so guarded, glowed a particular kind of warm. "At times...he smiles."

It looked like he was going to say more, but a flush colored his cheeks and he pushed to his feet as well, murmuring something unintelligible about 'tending to the fire.' The couple stared after him before Jesse leaned discreetly closer, speaking quietly into her ear.

"I have something for you as well. But I cannot give it to you here." He pulled in a breath, abruptly nervous, before tilting his head to the trees. "Would you take a walk with me?"

She stared at him in surprise. "Yes, alright."

He helped her to her feet and they left the little clearing, bidding the fae farewell, as they linked their arms together and headed off into the trees.

IT WAS A LONG TIME the couple walked together without speaking—never far apart, but never quite touching as well. While in the beginning they had been snugly intertwined, Jesse seemed to get more and more nervous the farther they strayed from camp, so thoroughly baffling Kiera with the sudden change, that they'd almost hiked a full mile before she reached out and caught his sleeve.

"Should we stop for food and water? Or is this present of yours close?"

He scanned manically over the terrain, feeling caged and claustrophobic despite the endless expanse, before returning to the girl beside him and coloring with a blush.

"No, here's...here's fine."

For what?

She watched as he unclasped his cloak, letting it ripple to the ground behind him. The boots were next, kicking lightly into the grass. "You're not going to kill me, are you?"

He leveled her with a choice look.

"I'm not accusing you," she said quickly, lifting her hands, "but you hear stories like that sometimes. Girl follows boy into forest. Boy has a change of heart, and strangles her to death."

On her birthday.

"I am not going to kill you," he said decisively, "no matter how the mood strikes. I actually just wanted to...there is this...this *thing* that I've been..." He let out a nervous breath, raking back his hair. "This would be so much easier if you were a shifter."

Kiera's face went still with surprise.

They never spoke of such things, though they were obvious enough. There were times he vanished into the forest, leaving his clothes behind. There were times when she heard a distant howl echoing off the trees. But shocking as those moments had been in the beginning, she was strangely accustomed to them now. There were some days when a part of her even forgot.

"Oh," she said quietly, fiddling with her hands. After a few seconds, she chanced another look at him. "Would you like me to pretend?"

His eyes flew up before he let out a burst of such loud laughter—it must have carried all the way back through the trees. The tension vanished and he closed the distance between them, taking her hands lightly in his own. A trace of a smile still lingered as he stared into her eyes.

"There is a custom, amongst my people. A custom that is known to every wolf, in every pack. It's a kind of...a kind of symbol, I guess. A surrendering between one person and other."

Her pulse quickened instinctively, though she didn't understand. "You wish me to...surrender to you?"

Again, on my birthday? Also, what does that mean?

"No," he said quietly, losing himself in her eyes. "Quite the other way around."

With her still watching, he took a deep breath and removed the rest of his clothing, stripping down to the barest and most vulnerable, until there was nothing left to his body but glowing, bronze skin. A flush crept into his cheeks, but he tried to steady himself—fingers trembling by his sides.

"They call it the binding. I've never known why." A breeze picked up around them, stirring the tips of his hair. "But you called us a couple the other day, and every couple I've ever known has done it. My parents did it. I always wondered if one day I'd do it myself."

By now, her pulse was racing at a speed that was probably unhealthy. His words had stacked atop each other, building the suspense and tension, until she couldn't possibly imagine the scope and scale of what might be coming next. But as it turned out, the act itself was rather simple.

With a final look, he shed his skin as well, disappearing in a blur of movement and color, until a chestnut, sleek wolf appeared in his place. It regarded her intently, staring with the exact same green eyes, before it walked quietly forward and pressed its nose to the ground at her feet.

She drew in a quick breath, staring down upon it.

She understood what he meant now, when he called it a surrender. And she understood why it was called the binding, for after that day, neither one of them would ever quite be the same. It was the greatest gift a person could give another. It was a piece of his heart. Offered freely, hers to keep.

She had never felt anything like it.

She would never feel anything like it again.

Chapter 6

Kiera and Jesse took their time in the forest, thinking of several more presents they could give one another, before eventually wandering back through the trees. The binding had been relatively chaste, compared to what happened next. The hours had crept along, and Kiera's cheeks were flushed and sore from laughing by the time they made it back into camp.

"Back so soon?" Eden teased, barely glancing up from his arrows. It was a habit he no longer noticed, an anxious fluttering of fingers to past the time. "I was about to search."

Kiera merely blushed and turned her face into Jesse's shoulder, while the shifter glanced swiftly around the camp. "Evander isn't back yet?"

The fae shook his head. His fingers moved faster.

"So the day is not yet done," Kiera said casually, easing down beside him. "It is still my birthday, you'll remember. A near-sacred day." Her fingers inched towards an arrow; he slapped down her hand. "I only mention it, because I have a question for you. One I've long wanted to ask."

Eden sighed quietly, but his lips curved with a smile. "Let's hear it, then."

She paused, like a diver preparing to jump. "How old are you?" She panicked the moment it left her lips, pairing it with an almost immediate, "I'm so sorry—is it terribly inappropriate for me to ask?"

He glanced towards her with a little smile. "Inappropriate?"

"I just mean...I would never want to offend you."

He laughed softly, returning to the arrows.

He had grown so practiced and checked them so many times, he no longer needed to look, though he often did. His fingers moved so quickly, she could scarcely see them in the fading light.

"You'd never want to offend me," he repeated under his breath. "I know for a *fact* that isn't true." But his eyes flicked up with a smile, catching the light. "Kiera, how old are you?"

There was a pause.

"...seventeen."

Eighteen, now.

"Are you offended?"

She blushed, then shook her head.

"The only thing that could be inappropriate is your reaction," he continued abruptly, almost warily, as if he'd been bracing just as long for the inevitable question. "In the context of mortality, these things tend to sound extreme—"

"Are you stalling, Eden?"

He threw her a look. "I'm close to nine hundred years old."

There was a beat of silence. Then—

"What?!"

A host of birds went screeching into the sky as her voice whipped across the clearing, striking loud enough to make her own teeth rattle, though she could feel nothing but surprise.

"Nine hundred?!" she shrieked, unable to do anything but repeat it. If he'd said ninety, it would have been enough. "But that's impossible! I mean, clearly not, but...that's *impossible*!"

He stiffened slightly, as though he'd been offended after all. "Why don't you think on it, while I fetch some more wood—"

She caught his sleeve as he made to stand, pulling him back down again. "Do you feel like it?" she asked eagerly.

"What do you mean?"

"Do you feel *nine hundred* years old?"

He sighed again, throwing a glance at the heavens. "This is why I warned of a hyperbolic reaction—"

"Hyperbolic reaction," she scoffed, still eyeing him like parts might suddenly break. "You are older than most trees." She shook her head, unable to wrap her mind around it. "But you are in your teens, perhaps your twenties. Aren't you? You and I, are we not technically aged the same?"

He eyed her speculatively, as if he'd never considered the question. "Possibly. I suppose we are not dissimilar."

Yes, we are.

"*Yes,* we are," she argued against herself, losing all concept of a filter. "We are about as dissimilar as two people can get. To start, I would never use a word like that on my own."

He opened his mouth to speak again, but she beat him to it.

"*Close* to nine hundred! You don't even bother counting anymore!" She shook her head incredulously, eyes widening to take up a ridiculous portion of her face. "And why would you...?"

By then, there was scarcely a need for the fae to be part of the conversation. He was the subject, little more, and she was more than capable of playing both parts herself.

"What will you do when you reach a thousand? Is there a ceremony of some kind?"

He frowned thoughtfully at the arrows before giving her a significant look. "At that point, the people who know me best would customarily turn my life into a play."

She couldn't tell if he was joking. Probably not.

"What's happened?" Jesse asked conversationally, joining them. He'd just returned from the trees, heaving another log onto the fire. "You look as though you've seen a ghost."

She scooted over quickly on the rocks to make room. "You know what? There's a chance that I have. I just asked Eden how old he was."

"Oh yes? How old?"

"It's really not important—" Eden tried to interject.

"He's *ancient*," she answered almost proudly. "He's close to nine hundred."

"Really." Jesse glanced at the fae with a little smile; there was a chance they'd already had a similar conversation. Then his eyes danced with sudden curiosity. "How old is Evander?"

Eden visibly stiffened, glancing with irritation at the shifter. "He's about the same age as me."

"About?" Kiera prompted eagerly.

"Give or take a decade."

She leaned back with a long breath as though she'd exhausted herself with the mere conversation. "So we truly do seem like children to you," she murmured. "How could we not?"

Eden regarded her a moment, then softened with a little smile. "The fae were entrusted with custodianship of this place. We were tasked with protecting. It is perhaps the reason we were granted immortality as well," he added, tendering as he looked upon her again. "Your age, especially when contrasted to mine...it makes that protecting very easy to do."

A gentle hush fell over the clearing, broken only by the soft fluttering and occasional crackle of the fire. The fae had a way of doing things like that. Seeing past the framework of such things, to the sweet intention beneath. It may have been unique to all his people, or perhaps just to himself.

The day's tasks were already finished, their bellies were sated, and the instruments they'd used had been properly stored and cleaned. There were little else to do but lose oneself in the hypnotic blaze of the fire. It was a long time before one of them finally broke the silence to speak.

"Where is he?" Eden muttered under his breath, glancing for the hundredth time around the shadowy woods. "I was expecting him back long ago."

Jesse followed his gaze, straightening a little upon the rock. "I believe he was hunting."

Eden nodded silently, but he did not look convinced.

If someone had asked before, Kiera might have believed there wasn't much in the forest that could do harm to a vampire. But the world wasn't the same placed it used to be. And seeing the worry on Eden's face, she suddenly wasn't sure.

"Would you like us to look for him?" Jesse asked softly.

It was a kind offer, one that might have embarrassed the fae if he'd been paying any attention. But he nodded faintly, gathering the arrows and pushing to his feet.

"Perhaps we should—"

There was a crackle in the trees behind them.

"There," Kiera interjected soothingly, "he is coming now."

She should have known it was wrong the moment she said it.

Why was she the one to have heard him? Why didn't one of the others hear it first? And why was she *able* to hear him? The vampire was perfectly silent, they could never hear him coming.

The ferns parted and a group of men stepped suddenly through the trees.

They had approached with almost as much stealth, though she didn't see how that was possible. They were the biggest, meanest, most heavily-armored men she had ever seen.

Not a vampire in sight.

CARPATHIANS.

Kiera didn't know the word until someone told her later. Never in her life had she seen a band of such brutes. Not even in the tavern, which was sometimes quite rough.

They seemed to swell the very air around them—too big for their clothing, too big for their swords. Most of them seemed mere playthings, though some had been forged to size. There was one battle-axe in particular that couldn't fail to catch the eye, sharpened wickedly on both sides.

And what of the others, she thought suddenly. *Such things weren't made for them, surely. But taken from others, people they've slain.*

There were nine of them, standing not in a group, but a loose line. As if they needed to take up more space. They had cut through the woods at a sudden angle, excited to see the smoke, but upon seeing the collection of people in front of them, it was impossible to hide their surprise.

"Good evening," the one in the middle spoke first, pairing the harsh grate of his voice with a gleaming smile. "I hope we did not interrupt your party."

Kiera stared blankly for a moment, then her eyes drifted over to where the picnic blanket was still stretched upon the ground. The dishes had been cleaned, but the food they'd decided to leave for the animals. When her eyes rested upon the honeyed flowers, she felt suddenly faint.

Eden had a singular focus, made even more pressing by the appearance of the men. "We are travelling with a vampire. Have you seen him?"

At first, she was surprised he'd asked so plainly. Then she was not. It was a dangerous thing, to risk angering a fae. And while these men might not be aware, it was also impossible to lie.

But the vampire was clearly a surprise.

"Are you really?" the Carpathian asked just as openly. "You?" He looked the fae slowly up and down. "That seems a rather unique arrangement. You must enlighten me."

As he spoke, more Carpathians poured through the trees, like the silent overturning of a glass. They strained the edges of the camp until it was no longer possible to see the forest behind them. She could feel the heat coming off their bodies. Dirt and blood, mixed with sweat.

"Another time," Eden said curtly. Outnumbered or not, the man's pride would allow him to speak no different. That being said, he wasn't foolish. He had been counting. And he did not like where things had ended up. "Where are you heading?"

"To the river countries," the man answered immediately, prompting a chortle of laughter from those behind them. "We're going to have a little fun..." He paused indulgently until it was quiet before continuing curiously. "What of yourselves? You are a long ways from anything."

The fae ignored the question, staring intently across the fire. "You would travel in this forest?"

It wasn't until he'd said it that Kiera realized it must be a particularly beloved wood. The fae gravitated towards places of serene, natural beauty and she had never been anywhere lovelier.

The man's lips twisted into a smirk.

"The fair folk do not patrol it as they once did. They are in their settlements now, preparing for a brighter future. We are concerned with the present, finding simple pleasures where we can."

His eyes strayed between them, lingering a moment on each one.

Jesse was completely unarmed, without even the small knife he carried as a precaution. Eden was holding a fist of arrows, but his bow was leaning against the side of the tent. If he had not been so foolishly distracted, worrying after the vampire, he might have grabbed it in time. And Kiera...?

The man wanted a closer look.

"Girl, bring us a drink." He planted his fists upon his hips, leaning backward slightly as the men laughed behind him. "Is this any way for a hostess to treat her guests?"

Strangely enough, it wasn't terribly different from commands she'd been given her entire life. Men liked giving commands, it was something she'd learned early on. And those commands were always loudest when they had an audience. But this man wanted something far more than a drink.

"Do not speak to her," Jesse answered through gritted teeth. His hand drifted towards his side, though nothing was there. "If you and your men are thirsty, I suggest you go elsewhere."

The Carpathian smiled and stepped forward as if he'd been hoping the shifter would say that exact thing. "Ah, but my men and I are tired as well. Long have we already travelled, and there is much farther still to go." His eyes glinted in the firelight. "What we really need, is a bed—"

At that point, several things happened.

Kiera reeled back as the man lunged forward. Jesse appeared in between. Weapon or not, he rammed into the Carpathian, forcing him back. He was caught himself in the process. Two men seized his arms before passing him back to their leader. A knife appeared, lodged beneath his throat.

Just seconds had passed. But they had changed everything.

"No."

Kiera gasped in horror, pulling against the grip that held her. The only reason she hadn't thrown herself straight back into the fray was that Eden had caught hold of her wrist.

He pulled her slowly behind him, never breaking the Carpathian's gaze.

"Let the boy go," he said softly, easing forward. "I am asking you."

Jesse strained against the fingers holding him. The dagger lifted his chin.

"Take her and leave," he hissed, unable to open his jaw. "You are faster than they are."

"That won't be necessary," Eden murmured, staking a step closer. His eyes alighted not on the dagger, but the man. "That is a mistake. He moved in defense of the girl. It was not to quarrel."

There was an edge of warning to his voice, but it was diplomatic all the same. This was not a fight he wanted. Though a fight seemed to be coming.

"I'm not sure if that matters," the man said lightly, digging around the tip of the blade with a grin. A few drops of blood peeked through the skin, spilling down his neck. "The boy attacked me."

Eden stopped at the blood, but raised his eyebrow with the hint of a smile.

"Do you *wish* to quarrel?"

There was an uneasy stirring amongst the Carpathians—all twenty of them, though they were facing only one man. But the smile was a front, Kiera had seen it before. Eden was stalling.

But stalling for what?

The man considered him for a long time, long enough that if her blood hadn't been spiked with fear, Kiera would have seen it as a compliment. Twice, his eyes drifted down to those long fingers. An archer's fingers. His people had felt their wrath many times before.

But the fae's bow was paces behind him. The boy would be dead by then.

"You are a long ways from anything," he murmured again, almost to himself. "You are burdened with mortals, in these woods alone." His own words seemed to convince him, he nodded their approval. "In light of present circumstances, I think we'll be taking that drink—"

"It appears we've forgotten our manners."

The vampire appeared out of nowhere, like a bolt from the sky. There were leaves in his dark hair, still fluttering skyward from the speed, but the rest of him was strangely motionless. He looked first, as always, to Eden. Then he turned those piercing eyes to the host of men before them.

Kiera sucked in a quick breath, half-thinking to see the ground scorched beneath his feet.

"You were not deceiving..." The rest of the Carpathians stopped their smiling. Even the man holding the dagger had the good sense to look afraid. "You are travelling with a vampire."

But Eden was no longer listening. He was staring at the back of Evander's head with a feeling of such overwhelming relief, for a moment, he could not breathe.

He recovered himself quickly, offering a tense greeting.

"We have visitors. Friends from Carpathia."

Evander nodded slowly, his eyes finding each one.

"I love Carpathians," he said softly, cocking his head with the ghost of a smile. "I love the sound they make when they fall."

There was not a breath in the clearing. Even the nighttime birds had the good sense not to speak. The man tightened his grip upon the blade, making Jesse arch backward into him.

"Careful, vampire," he warned, weighing his options at the same time. "Or I will split your friend from his head to his boots. I promise you, he will not look so pretty then."

Evander's voice was smooth and cold as a winter stream. "Touch a hair on his head, and they will find you in pieces."

It was perhaps the most frightening thing about vampires. A race so utterly devoid of natural predators, they were not build with the concept of a bluff. The Carpathian clearly knew this, his men were angling for the trees. But those eternal eyes had already found each one of them.

And vampires were also not built to forgive.

Eden took a step freely into the open, not towards the tent with all his weapons, but towards their visitors instead. They had brought enough weapons. Several of them were just his size.

"Jesse...I wish you were not wearing shoes."

The two men locked eyes for a split second. The calm before the storm.

Then that storm was upon them.

There was a sound like a blacksmith's wheel, as flesh ripped from flesh, and the cries that followed lost themselves in the night air. They were an emblem, the final burst of life. Like the smoke an extinguished candle leaves behind. It would be remembered just briefly, then forgotten.

Almost before anything else, Jesse had disappeared from the fight altogether—making the transformation mid-air, as his body flipped backward, landing behind the Carpathian line. Whether it was what he'd intended or merely the only angle he could jump without losing his neck, the others would never know. But Kiera suspected the former. The *boy*, as the others so been so distractedly referring to him, might have been a mere twenty years old, but he carried the pride of a wolf.

And he was more than capable of fighting back.

There was a sweet sting of metal, as he disarmed the first man standing in front of him, and ran the second through with his blade. The third gave him little more challenge, lunging foolishly for a feigned parry and impaling himself in the process. And by the time the fourth had turned around, Jesse had already slipped right through that clanking armor, blood dripping from his blade.

The others were engaging in an equally direct approach.

Eden had never gone back for the bow, but he was still using the arrows. Like an animal that had sprouted sudden claws, he leapt upon anyone who tried to stop him—finding the weak points in their armor, and silencing the first flickers of resistance with deadly, lightning-fast jabs. Whenever someone began to crowd him or venture too near, he kicked them back again—imperious as ever, even when dealing those lethal blows. They would be patient. They would wait their turn.

Evander was fighting beside him—never too close, but never too far. There was something just as compelling, but harder to trace. The vampire was simply there, and then he wasn't. No blurring spirals of motion, no shimmering arcs of light. He was death, working with light fingers.

It was the moments he slowed down that were the most troubling. When he took his time.

"Please!"

There came a wailing cry as a man inched along the ground—staring up with a look of sheer terror, as he retreated in slow motion from the vampire. While there was no way of him knowing, it was the first time a Carpathian had ever said the word. His palms slipped on the slick grass, shaking with such visceral fear, the others could smell the stench.

"No—please!"

There was something strange about saying *please* to a vampire. Like shouting at the clouds to stop the rain. Still the man tried, wracked with dry, choking sobs that brought no air.

Evander stared down without expression. A cold god amongst the trees.

Instead of snapping the man's neck, as he'd done with so many others, instead of simply crushing his skull as he walked by, the vampire knelt down instead, reaching towards him.

There was a soft intake of breath as he kept reaching. And kept reaching still further after that. His fingers vanished, then came up bright red. An unnatural color, different from all the rest.

He leaned forward with a whisper, lips touching the man's ear. "Pick better friends."

So many there had been when the friends had started, and so few there were just a few moments in. There had been a few injuries, sacrifices of their own blood. But considering the size and admitted skill that battled against them, there was no shame in any one.

Jesse got a fist to the jaw that sent him stumbling into the shadows, seeing stars. Eden got a slice across the back of the shoulder, a warm sting and the air was scented with blood.

There had been retribution then, but not by the fae's own hand.

No sooner had the vampire's head snapped up across the clearing, than the man in question was lying in four separate pieces—each one pointing with odd symmetry in a different direction, like a gruesome compass that couldn't make up its mind.

Not one of them had made it to Kiera. Not a single one.

She had dutifully done what she always did, what they always told her to do. She had run a safe distance, and proceeded to hide. How she hated herself in those moments when her mortality stung worse than an adder's bite, and she had to watch from a distance as the ones she loved battled to stay alive. Sometimes she found herself wanting to call out and warn them. On countless different occasions, she'd sprung to her feet to join them, desperate to throw herself into the fight.

But almost as if by uncanny intuition, one of them would always glance her way. Her cheeks would flush and she would sink back into the shadows, remembering her place the way a child was taught to remember its name.

I am a mortal. I have no special powers. I am unskilled with a blade.

The adrenaline would fade, the shame would set in, and the inevitable reality would tighten her chest. She would not be a help, but a hindrance. The greatest thing she could do was hide—

"There you are!"

She whipped around with a gasp, staring at the gruesome man who'd demanded she bring him a drink just a few minutes before. His shoulder was bleeding and he was missing a large chuck of hair, but aside from that, he seemed to have deserted the fight a great deal sooner than his men.

Brave man, hiding behind his friends. Her chest tightened. *Brave like you.*

She threw a quick glance over her shoulder, but the others were engaged in fights of their own and not a single of them looked her way. She had chosen her spot well, deep in the ravine that ran alongside the camp. Her body was tilted almost straight vertical, allowing her a glimpse of what was happening, while having the option to scramble away in case she was seen.

At least, that had been the idea.

"There is time for you to run," she whispered. "They might not find you."

It was the only leverage she had and he probably should have taken it. Their distraction would not last forever; they would be coming for her before long.

But Carpathians were not built for such mercies. They were built to make people scream.

"I will leave," he conceded, bleeding freely down the face. "But I'm taking you with me."

She cried out when he grabbed for her, flipping onto her stomach and falling against the slope. Her fingers scrambled in the bramble for anything she might use to help, but came away twisted in vines and smeared with blood. There was a great pressure behind her, pushing her so deep into the mountain, it felt as though she couldn't breathe. Her lungs ached for air, heaving in silence, while his fingers twisted against her scalp, coming up with a fist of hair.

There was a sharp tug and the ground vanished beneath her. Her hands clawed desperately at the open air, grabbing hold of anything they could find.

It was her birthday flowers. The ones from Evander.

Without stopping to think, she twisted around and shoved them into the Carpathian's face, holding them steady, as he drew in a great breath of surprise. When his mouth opened, she pushed them inside, screaming like a feral creature, cramming them with every bit of force she could muster, until all at once she realized...the man was no longer alive.

She let out a final shriek and jerked backward, watching in belated terror as he slid down the front of her dress and fell with a splat in the mud. There was a dull impact, then everything went perfectly still. So much movement a second before, then perfectly, incomprehensibly still.

That was when she heard a sound and looked at the ridge above her. A small group of people had gathered. Three sets of dirty faces. Three pairs of glittering eyes.

"I don't understand," Evander said in confusion. "Did he choke?"

Jesse shook his head, still trying to catch his breath. "The flowers you gathered—they're poisonous."

Evander shot him a look of surprise, then hopped down into the clearing. He ignored Kiera completely and knelt down beside the corpse, its mouth still twisted open in a silent scream. Without a moment's pause, he reached inside and pulled out a crumpled petal, running it between his fingers.

A second later, his face lightened with a sudden memory.

"You know what? I'm pretty sure I knew that."

Chapter 7

Three days went past. Then three more after that.

The friends made their way steadily up the range of mountains, making only brief stops, walking until the moon had already risen high above them. Some were trying hard to forget the bodies they'd left behind them. Some had not remembered past the first slopes.

It was on a rare evening they'd stopped before dusk that Kiera was sitting by herself a short ways from the others, arms curled around her knees, a faint frown upon her face. The sky was full of meadow-larks, up later than usual and calling loud throughout the trees. It was a lilting song, lovely.

It irritated her. Everything irritated her. She was irritated by the sky itself.

"She is quiet," Eden whispered loudly, stoking the embers of a wilting fire. "It is never a good sign when she's quiet."

The three men were seated together, their backs against a smooth crop of rocks stretching above them onto a grassy plain. The journey had been full of contradictions like that. Trees one moment and fields the next. The seams were not so woven together, but jagged and extreme.

She got up in one swift movement, pacing towards them. "I need you to teach me to fight."

She aimed it not at either of the others, but directly at the fae. The one from whom she'd first extracted a promise. The one she thought would be most likely to help.

His eyes fixed upon her in surprise, bright with curiosity. "Of course, I have already agreed to that." He pushed halfway to his feet. "It has been a while since our last lesson—"

"Not placate me, *teach* me."

Those feelings of helplessness swelled inside her once again. It had taken her three days of walking to realize there was anger at the core. This would not be a thing that would come to define her. She would not be safe-guarded and scripted onto the side. She would stand beside her brothers.

They would take up arms together.

"Teach me with the same frustration you might feel, if all your life you'd been expected to sit on the edge of a fight." She shook her head, bouncing in place. "I'm not doing that anymore."

The men stared up in unison, their expressions frozen.

After a few seconds, Jesse cleared his throat.

"We asked you only because—"

"You asked me only because I don't know any better."

"You killed someone—"

"I killed him with flowers! Do not get me started!"

Eden nodded slowly, solemn and sincere. "I understand. I agree with you. But do not discount the things you've already done," he continued gently. "You have come far, Kiera. In a short time, you have learned much—"

"You have given me some basic skills, I'll not deny that. But in the end, those skills amount to the same courage as a deserter, ready to sacrifice his friends." Her voice rose in timbre. "You have been easy on me, you have listened to my whining, and I will *never* be prepared!"

The fae flinched, then froze very still. "It was never my intention—"

"The best of intentions kill women in the forest," she said briskly. "I need better than intentions now. Please, Eden. Get to your feet."

The fae got to his feet.

The others did as well, following in silence up the rocks and to the grassy plain above. The evening sun cast slanting shadows across the lawn, like pointed fingers reaching towards them. It was not the best time to be sparring, Kiera knew this. The shading was at its most difficult, and it was hard to see the fae's attacks coming in the best of light.

So far, their training had been in stolen moments of broad daylight, with everything illuminated to its best. But that evening, she didn't care.

The Carpathians had come at dusk. The light had been the same.

"We shall pick up where we left off," the fae said quietly, looking almost uneasy to have an audience. "An actual fight, no scripted movements. But slow, Kiera. Keep it slow."

She nodded at top-speeds, forgetting the concept of *slow*.

When the fae inclined his head, she flew towards him—taking advantage of his moment of surprise to kick him straight in the chest. He fell back a step, letting out a sharp breath. But he didn't stop her. At least, he didn't make *her* stop. He simply adjusted his own movements so they suited her pace, battling across the field at whatever speed she might like.

"Remember your arm," he instructed, ducking as she curled it towards his face. "Good, now in this position"—he flipped her lightly onto the grass, changing mid-thought—"*don't* do that, *never* do that. It's a sure-fire way to get yourself—"

"What, applauded?" She picked herself up with a glare, dusting off the grass. "I'm fairly sure that's from a *waltz*, Eden. This isn't teaching me."

He threw up his hands. "Then what would you have me do?

"How did *you* learn to fight?" she countered, looking from one to the other. "You grew up fighting. Your whole lives...you've been fighting, while I've been serving you drinks! It is time I got *my* share of the fighting! And that's not going to happen with you treating me like a doll."

She struck him across the face. Hard. "Now me."

He went still as a deer. "What?"

"*Hit* me." She gestured to her face, teeth grinding together. "Hit me the same way it would actually happen. Hit me the same way you would do to anyone else."

Jesse stepped forward, tensed to the brink. "Kiera, you can't ask him to do that—"

"This is why I didn't come to *you* for help. Do it, Eden. No more coddling, no more acting like we're just playing pretend. I'm sure it hurt the first time someone hit you, too. Now hit me."

His hand lifted slowly, then lowered back to his side.

"You can't ask me to do that," he said softly.

A hard silence stretched between them, louder than anything that had come before. Beneath that endless sky, there seemed no hiding from it, no escaping it. It threatened to consume them all.

Evander lifted his hand. "I can do it."

Three people turned in silence. Three people spoke at the same time.

"*What?*"

"*What!*"

"*What!?*"

The vampire shrugged casually, hands in his pockets. "I will teach the girl."

And the cat would play games with the bird. And the fox and lamb would curl up together, intuiting bedtime stories and falling asleep. So the vampire would give sparring lessons to a mortal.

"That is a joke," Eden said flatly, no hint of a question.

"It is not," Evander countered. "I have been fighting for just as long as you, perhaps even longer. Why could I not instruct her—"

"The fae misspoke," Jesse interrupted sharply, "that is a *bad* joke, Evander. The kind of joke you should not be making again."

The vampire's lips twitched in a faint smile. "Do you think me lacking in control?"

The fae blushed and turned his eyes.

"Kiera has nothing to fear. I will check my strength."

Her eyes flashed up when he said her name. Usually she was *the girl*, or *the mortal*, or on particularly bad days, *the one with the red hair*. Seldom was she Kiera.

But she was that day.

"You will not eat me?" she asked shrewdly.

He lifted his hand in such a boyish gesture, it took everything in her not to laugh. Their eyes met, and all at once, she was abruptly convinced the vampire would be the person she'd always ask.

"Then let us begin."

He flew towards her without another word, slowing down just enough that she was able to see it coming, which in hindsight was much worse. By the time she'd lifted her hands, she was sprawling across the grass, striking the ground with enough force all the air rushed from her chest.

Eden winced in silence..

Jesse simply closed his eyes "I cannot watch this," he muttered.

"You would have laughed if it was Eden," she answered, picking herself back up. A knot swelled on the back of her head, and her mouth tasted bloody. "You'd laugh if it was yourself."

...which is baffling...

The world might have been spinning, but she put on a good façade. As soon as it tilted back on its axis, she paced calmly forward, lifting both her hands. "How can I stop something like that? If someone just charges towards me, how can I avoid ended up on my back?"

Evander lifted his eyebrows, almost mocking. "You need to understand that *I'm* not going to stop."

Right.

The next time he came at her, she flew even farther.

Though she did have a slightly better idea what to expect.

From that point on, it became clear that Evander didn't mean to give her a lesson. He meant simply to fight her, a lesson in itself. Instead of the patient lecture and repetition, *endless* repetition, of the others, he moved at whim from one moment to the next, from one attack to the next. It seemed to be not so much about the fight, but merely understanding the mindset of a fighter.

At the core of Evander, there was nothing but confidence.

He knew his body, he knew what it could do. When facing down an opponent, he knew exactly what to expect. It was perhaps the reason vampires were so choosy when picking fights. That unholy strength and fantastical speed were grounded by simple pragmatism. A dark anchor to steady the lightning flashes of those hands. It was a valuable lesson, though their standards were different.

At the core of Kiera, there was nothing but sheer will.

It was something she had not known until the question was put upon her. A fundamental piece of humanity that had been unable to ever thrive. It was what kept the fight going, kept her getting off the ground. It was what kept her driving at her opponent, searching for new ways to attack him, waiting for the inevitable moment, no matter how far away, that she finally got through.

That moment will not be today.

There was a high-pitched shriek as he struck her across the face—using precisely the same amount of force as when she'd hit Eden. The shadows blossomed and stars burst behind her eyes. It took a few seconds, before she was fully able to come back.

"Now me," he commanded.

Her hand flew up of its own accord, fueled with a dizzied rage she'd never known. But it stopped just as fast, stuck mid-air like a sudden wind had risen against it, making her unable to fully connect. The dissonance was overwhelming. She could not be damaging. She could not be rude. The impulse swelled inside her, but it was like trying to flex a muscle that wasn't there.

She struck him anyway, a sharp slap across the face. One meant to dissuade. His hair flew back, but his face was steady. When those dark locks had settled, he tilted his head with a little smile.

"That is not how I struck you."

Her cheeks flamed and she nodded quickly. "I know. Sorry, I just—"

"Do you think I would ever *apologize* for something like that? Do you think people often apologize when doing such things?" He looked at her intently. "There is a difference between mercy and apology. One is to be used at your discretion. There is no place for the other here."

She nodded again, but kept her eyes on the ground, still flushed with a growing sense of shame she could not begin to unravel. A kind of weight had descended upon her shoulders, making her feel heavy and exposed, as if her body was taking up too much space beneath the endless sky.

This was a mistake. This is indulgent. I should not have asked for this.

He regarded her intently another moment, almost as if he was listening along. Then he slipped his fingers beneath her chin and lifted it until the two were eye to eye.

"Until you make it real, it never will be," he spoke softly, but there was a thrill in those quiet words, as thrilling as the vampire himself. "If you want something, you must take it."

She drew in a breath and struck him. *Actually* struck him. There was a crack like she had never heard and she yanked her hand back almost immediately, fingers stinging like a burn.

He considered. "...that was not very good."

Her arm dropped to her side. He lifted it with a coaxing smile.

"It will get better. Try again."

She swung at him again, but found herself stymied by a new impulse—holding back even as she was swinging, her fingers still throbbing, forbidding herself to wield such force. "I don't wish to hurt you."

"You don't wish to fail."

"No," she insisted, "I don't wish to hurt you."

Time stilled between them, as she suddenly realized this was the crux. Not just the pain, but the risk to both sides. There was a cost to such exposure. There was a fear in removing the net.

"You will not hurt me," he answered, quiet but firm. "I am not the kind to bend or waver. I am not the kind to break. Let us see the best you have to offer."

His eyes flicked up for a split second, drifting somewhere over her shoulder.

"Test that strength out on me."

She threw herself upon him a second later, battering with her fists and grasping with all her might, abandoning every trace of caution and wisdom and restraint. There was pain. Such unending, unsupervised pain, she thought she might never feel whole again. But there was such freedom there as well. As if every other moment had been stunted. As if some invisible pressure had been lifted, and for the first time in her life, she was able to use her lungs properly, to take a deep, filling breath.

"That's better!" Evander called, rising up to meet her. "Again!"

The shifter was cheering, soon he would join in. But he was the only one.

The fae had gone very still at the edge of the clearing, freezing as if the vampire's words had been meant for his ears alone. He stood the rest of the lesson in silence. Watching them go through the paces. Watching the devastating and delicate way the vampire handled his friends.

When it was finished, he paced into the trees and didn't return for a long time.

Chapter 8

The friends travelled on with a slightly different dynamic than before.

When they set out upon the trail, Kiera often took the lead—with one of the others walking alongside her. As they went, they would speak of others things than she was used to. The best way to fend off bandits. The little signs that gave away the fragile crust of a washed out trail.

Safety, for the others.

When they settled beside the fire each night, things were different as well.

She felt as if someone had replaced her, like the body attached was no longer her own. Just a few short days under the tutelage of the vampire and it was already beginning to change, smoothing in parts and angling in others, always waking quicker than before. The effect was delightful, yet the balance of pain was equally strong, like someone had taken a giant hammer to all the most delicate parts of her, banging them into sudden focus, muscles and tendons she never knew existed before.

She would not have traded the time for anything. But such change was never easy. And she was not the only one caught in the flux of something she didn't fully understand.

"Is your shoulder all right?"

The vampire had asked the same question since a Carpathian swordsman had sliced the fae with his blade. It was not very deep, and had mostly healed already. But the question came each day.

Eden nodded in silence, flexing his fingers. As if to prove it, he reached absentmindedly for his arrows, although they hadn't been recently used, and began his nightly check.

Things had settled into a quiet rhythm between the immortals. One pushing ever so slightly, as the other pulled ever so slightly back. It was a tired balance, yet impeccably maintained. But Jesse was right about them watching each other. And it wasn't just the vampire watching the fae.

There were moments when Eden would find himself staring at Evander, his eyes fixed on that inscrutable face. What he was thinking, no one could guess. It was likely the fae scarcely knew himself. But he no longer looked away when the vampire caught him staring. They would simply regard each other in silence, like each one was trying to pry secrets from the other's head.

Then one day, it seemed looking was no longer enough.

"Are we ever going to talk about it?" Evander asked suddenly. "The day I kissed you?"

The others froze what they were doing, as the fae glanced up in shock. It was a rather key component of the aforementioned balance. But the vampire was taking a hammer to that as well.

"I have thought on it often enough," he continued quietly, staring across the fire. "Walking beside you all day. Sleeping beside you all night. It rarely leaves my mind."

A flushed silence fell between them, hot as a dragon's breath.

"We should go," Jesse muttered, pushing halfway to his feet. "Give you a little—"

Eden's hand flew out and caught him. "No—stay."

Never had quite such a command been given. Yet the same words had been whispered to friends around campfires since the dawn of time. The fae blushed, then continued quickly.

"There is no need to discuss such things, and no need for you to remember." His eyes fell upon the vampire. "I have given my answer, the matter is settled."

Move on.

The words he *didn't* say echoed just as loud in the clearing, stiffening the others and ringing in Evander's ears. But instead of taking them to heart, the vampire offered a sweet smile in return.

"For now."

Kiera was frozen in such comedic astonishment, it was a blessing that no one happened to look her way. A dented spoon was lifted halfway to her mouth, tilting precariously, and she did not notice when it began to spill. She *could not believe* he was being so bold. *Could not believe it.*

Eden had no idea what to make of it. He simply returned to his arrows.

He kept losing count.

"Do you remember that tune the bards were singing?" Evander continued after a long while, speaking to no one in particular. "The bards I most definitely did *not* eat." He paused a moment, as if giving the others an opportunity to challenge it. "Kiera—do you remember how it went?"

She flushed to have been singled out, but shook her head. There was a dollop of stew on the ground beside her. She nudged some dirt over it with the tip of her boot.

The vampire stretched back with an untroubled expression, humming a few notes under his breath. They hung sweetly in the air, like the chimes of a bell. Lovely, yet incomplete.

"That's not it," he murmured, turning to Eden. "Surely you remember. I can think only of the pleasure it gave you. The brightness of your smile. I cannot believe you would forget."

The fae set down his arrows slowly, unwilling to count again from the start. "I do not wish to speak of this."

"Then we shall speak of something else," the vampire said cheerfully. "There was a wren on the trail the other day that reminded me of you, perched on a tree in perfect stillness, except when it opened its mouth to sing. It flew away when my shadow fell over it. I was sorry to see it go."

Eden stared in silence, fingers itching for his bow.

"Or perhaps I shall remind you of my better qualities, in case you have begun to forget. I have saved your life on numerous occasions. I have stopped myself from eating the children more times than I will ever admit." Evander spoke like it was just the two of them, ticking things off on his hands, stoking at the tension like the embers of a fire. "I am quiet on the trail, and keep watch better than the rest. And while you have no way yet to know it, I am also an exceedingly good—"

Eden pushed abruptly to his feet, sweeping from the clearing without a backwards glance.

The others stared after him without moving, without even breathing, as if some spell had rooted them to the spot. After a minute had passed, Kiera turned with accusation to Evander.

"Is that what you wanted?"

His eyes stayed fixed upon the trees. "It is a start."

EDEN SWEPT GRACEFULLY through the forest without a clear thought as to where he was going, propelled only by a rush of feeling—one that had become too powerful to ignore. Too long, he had tried to contain it. His body ached with the effort. Like trying to hold back a rising tide.

He had walked away, he told himself. He had not fled.

But he wasn't sure it mattered. The end result was the same.

His only consolation were the woods themselves, painted gold in the fading sunset, laced with the same patterns and scents he'd known as a boy. He peered through their blazing canopy to the sun itself, letting it burn the backs of his eyes. A stab of pain rushed through him, followed by a sightless oblivion. He stared a moment longer, trembling, like a new sword pulled from the fire.

How many times had he sought refuge in just such a place, finding comfort in the easy song of the birds, the gentle rush of the stream? Each of his people took solace in those simple beauties, but to him, they had become a true sanctuary. Always another ridge in the distance, always another peak to climb. *Movement.* He had become addicted. His friends had chuckled it off as an obsession. His lovers had fallen in priority, before drifting away. He was always relieved to be alone again. The beat of his own heart, the rhythm of his own feet. It had been the same way since he was a child.

There was a rush of air behind him. He closed his eyes against the burn.

"What do you want, Evander?"

Of course the man had followed him. He'd been following him without mercy for over a month, shadowing his footsteps, haunting his dreams. Why should tonight be any different? When he didn't receive an answer, he cracked open his eyes, only to see the vampire standing in front of him. He stood like an ivory spear against all that flaming color, his black hair was burnished gold.

Those eyes found him as they always did. Tracing him slowly up and down.

"You know what I want."

The words settled inside him like a stone, dragging him further from that protection. He stared for a moment, unable to comprehend its grip, then shook his head in wonder.

"Why do you speak to me this way?"

Evander paused, like he had not expected to be asked. After a few trailing moments, he replied the same way as the last. "You know why."

The fae tensed slightly, like the answer had disappointed him. "You have my word on that."

Evander ground his jaw together, straining the edge of his patience. "Perhaps I cannot leave it—"

"Try bloody harder." Eden opened his mouth to say something else, flushed with anger, ready for the fight, but the sight of Evander wilted him just as fast. He turned to face a different direction, pressing his wrist to his forehead, as if the mere idea was enough to cause him physical pain.

"Just leave," he breathed, "please. I cannot...I cannot do this with you."

Whether he meant the conversation or something more, it was unlikely either of the men would never know. But the vampire stood his ground.

"You look for me the same way I look for you. In a fight. In the morning." He took a step closer. "You were stalling with the Carpathians, hoping I would get to you in time."

Eden threw up his hands, whipping back around. "You are a vampire, and we were outnumbered. *Yes*, I was hoping you'd return. I thought we were all about to die—"

"You are never happier than when you think you're about to die," Evander interrupted sharply before cooling with a smile. "It is one of the reasons we might do so well together."

Eden let out a hard breath of laughter.

"Is this a seduction?" His bright eyes glimmered in the fading light, both a warning and a challenge. "Or perhaps you think there is no reason for that. Do not think I've forgotten the things you and Jesse said. He was taunting you. He said you could kill the pair of them and simply *have* me. His words." The fae paused. "You *agreed* with him." He paused again. "Do you agree with him still?"

"Is that why you've been angry?" Evander asked in surprise. "Is that the reason for your hesitation? You think I do not wish to offer you a choice? Or that I have limited your options somehow? Of *course* I wish for you to choose, it is the *reason* I have kept asking the question."

"And I have given you my answer," Eden shot back, "still you persist." He shook his head, quoting bitterly under his breath. "Limited my options..." He stepped forward abruptly, fists balled at his sides. "You attacked me, *bit* me, stalked me, then attacked me again. Since you nearly killed me in the forest, you have haunted my every thought. I believed I was going mad when I continued to see you amongst the trees. Thank the gods the others could see you too!"

He was breathing very quickly, chest moving up and down.

"I allowed you to stay. I staked you upon my honor. I gave you my trust and placed the lives of my friends in your hands. Now you would ask *this* of me as well?" His voice rose uncontrollably until he finished in a near-shout. "You are...you are *everywhere*, Evander! I see nothing else each waking moment! You have made yourself the *only* choice!"

The vampire stepped back, struck silent as a ghost.

In a way, it was the greatest declaration of feeling he could have received. Shouted in anger, surrendered in a fit of rage. Truth be told, it was a rather standard reaction for a fae.

When he finally answered, it was quiet. A stark contrast.

"I ask nothing beyond what you already desire."

"And what do you know of my desires?" Eden shouted, throwing up his hands. "What makes you claim to know my heart better than I know it myself?"

Evander's eyebrows lifted, like he had given something away. "A fae who doesn't know his own heart?" he quipped. "Quite the conundrum."

"You are overstepping. This has gone too far."

"We have not even started."

Eden threw up his hands again and walked away. At least, he tried. No sooner had he taken three steps, than Evander was already standing in front of him again, holding him by the wrists.

"Do not touch me—"

"Stop walking away."

They squared against each other, flushed and panting. Even the vampire, who was usually so cool, found the blood racing in his veins.

But there was something about the fae's expression that reminded him very much of that bird in the branches. He was suddenly afraid he'd take flight.

"I do not wish to upset you," he said softly. "Truly, Eden. That is the last thing I wish."

The fae stood trembling before him, white-faced with rage. "Then what do you *want* from me? What must I do?"

Evander regarded him a moment, then his face softened with the hint of a smile. "I want to kiss you again. I want you to kiss me."

Eden cursed in frustration, storming away once more. "You are relentless—"

The vampire grabbed him by the shoulders, shoving him into the base of a tree. There was a brief struggle, followed by several more choice profanities, but the fae was unable to escape.

"Let go," he demanded, still trying to free himself. "Don't *touch* me."

The word struck between them, loud and sharp—and tinged with something different, a distant kind of pain. Like an old wound that never healed right, one that stung when mishandled.

Evander took a step back, staring deep into his eyes.

"When I drank your blood, it created a bond between us. Something that will last as long as we do. Something that can be ended only by death."

Eden stared back in disbelief. "What are you talking about?"

"I can feel the things you're feeling. I can follow where you go." Evander took a breath to steady himself, as if he'd never discussed such things out loud. "It is exceedingly rare—"

"That's madness. There is no such thing."

"Is it possible to lie to a fae?"

Eden went frightfully quiet.

"When you told me there were things you could not give," Evander continued softly, "you meant it." He paused. "But a part of you wanted to. A part of you wants me to kiss you right now."

The fae shook his head like he could ward it away. "No," he began shakily, "I don't want to see you anymore."

"If that was true, I would be gone," the vampire murmured, stepping closer. "I would leave tonight and you would never see me again. But you *want* this. I can feel it. That thing you've refused to name, the one you've forbidden to yourself—I can *feel* that."

A rendering. A fact.

It occurred to the fae in that moment, perhaps he had fled after all.

And perhaps it had mattered a great deal.

"You want this," Evander whispered again, a quiet affirmation.

The two locked eyes, then he leaned in with a sudden kiss.

Their faces tumbled awkwardly together, like the pieces of two very different puzzles, trying to find a way to fit. When Evander touched Eden's shirt, sliding a smooth hand along the lines of his stomach, Eden shivered and pulled away, his back pressed roughly against the tree.

"This is too much," he breathed, trying to steady himself. A part of him was desperate for the vampire to hear it. Another part was just as desperate for him to disagree. "Something as great as this..." He forced Evander to look him in the eyes. "There could be no coming back from it."

The vampire let out a burst of laughter.

"You're such an optimist," he mused affectionately, tucking back a strand of the fae's bright hair. "You think there's any coming back?"

The vampire kissed him again, hands sliding out of sight, finding the clasps on clothing, as shirts began falling one after another to the forest floor. It wasn't until a breeze picked up that Eden leaned away suddenly, still unsure whether he wanted it to happen. He froze in a split second of indecision, wavering, then he reached forward and ran both hands through Evander's dark hair.

He caught his breath, then smiled.

I've wanted to do that a long time.

They grabbed each other at the same time—bodies pulling together, fingers tangling into hair. Their lips crushed together, hungry and bruising, and when each of them took a simultaneous step forward, the ground slipped out beneath them and sent both tumbling to the forest floor.

They laughed a moment, blushed and panting, before finding their way more slowly into each other's arms. Eden brushed some leaves from the vampire's hair. Evander wiped a smear of dirt from his cheek. Their lips were almost touching, when Eden pulled back with a whisper.

"Don't bite me."

The vampire grinned and pulled him closer. "I make no promises."

Chapter 9

Eden and Evander didn't come back to camp that night. Neither were they to be found the morning after. The others saw no trace of them until the following afternoon.

"Wonderful," Jesse grumbled under his breath, "here they come..."

The shifter had slept poorly, tossing and turning all through the night. He had been restless that morning as well—trying to busy himself with the day's tasks. But no sooner would he start, than he'd stop abruptly and with no seeming provocation—glaring in frustration at the distant trees.

It wasn't until the immortals returned that Kiera understood why.

Oh...right.

Eden was *glowing*.

She had grown used to a certain level of radiance from the fae, a predictable degree of heavenly beauty. But never had she seen him lit up in such a way. It was impossible to look at anything else. The only one who might have matched him, was the vampire at his side.

Evander looked happy, but tired.

He was relaxed in a way she had never seen, one that made him all the more irresistible. No longer was he searching for the fae, the man was walking alongside him. His eyes flicked over every so often just to be sure, the hollows beneath them bruised with the faintest of shadows.

She wasn't surprised. Fae were known for their endurance.

"Good morning!" Eden called brightly, as they approached.

Her lips pursed, as she lifted a hand. "Good afternoon."

The vampire swept past them towards the pile of kindling, gathering the makings of a fire, while Eden breezed quickly in the opposite direction—heading straight for the tent.

"How was your night?" Jesse asked dryly, as he passed.

"Oh, you know...fine." He vanished a second later behind the door.

Jesse's eyes hardened and he reached theatrically for the hilt of his sword. Kiera swatted down his hand with a giggle, pulling him back and speaking under her breath.

"It's sweet," she whispered. "Why must you have a problem with it?"

He ground his teeth in irritation, raking back his hair. "You could not hear them so clearly as I," he muttered. "It was *ceaseless.*"

"It's *sweet,*" she said again, more sternly this time. "They like each other. They have liked each other for a long while. Why must there be something wrong in it?"

They watched as the vampire smiled to himself, splitting apart a log with his bare hands. The two pieces fell soundlessly to the ground, rolling themselves still. Jesse held back a shudder.

"Why, indeed."

They lingered a moment longer before slipping inside the tent themselves.

In hindsight, it was quite possible the fae was hoping for a few minutes of privacy in the hopes of being discreet. When they came inside, he was in the process of changing his clothes.

...and it was a sight to behold.

"Seven hells!" Jesse exclaimed, yanking away his tunic.

The fae's usually smooth skin was marked with a dozen slender crescents—vampiric bites that covered him from head to toe. They weren't very deep, but they were everywhere. His neck and both wrists. The side of his ribs, the curve of his shoulder. The top of his hip.

He snatched the shirt back with a glare, pulling it over his head. "Leave, or I'll shoot you."

"Don't strain yourself," Jesse answered with a grin. He seemed to be having a much easier time with things, now that he realized the fae's evening had come at a price. "You've lost a lot of blood, Eden. You need to gather your strength—"

The fae reached for his bow, and Jesse vanished like a ghost.

Kiera waited until the tent fluttered shut behind him, and she and the fae were alone. Then she caught Eden's arm ever so gently, drawing her fingertips around a bite on the side of his hand.

"...does it hurt?" she asked shyly.

He hesitated, then glanced down with the trace of a smile. "Precisely the right amount."

She flushed with a grin and released him, casually straightening the rumpled blankets as he finished getting dressed. He might have lost just as much blood as the shifter had teased, but his eyes were bright and his movements were quick as ever. In only a few seconds, he was finished.

"Are you ready?" he asked over his shoulder—waiting for some reason, though his eyes were already glued to the thin crack of light. "You two haven't eaten yet, have you?"

She shook her head, crossing to his side.

"No, we haven't eaten." She reached for the door, then hesitated, trying her best to hold back the question. After a second, she flashed him a quick look. "How are you not...?" She couldn't say frightened. If she said frightened, he would never let her live it down. "...concerned?"

He regarded her fondly, eyes warming with a smile. "If I didn't do something every time I was concerned, I'd have never left Farion. I would never have even gotten to Farion. I'd still be feasting with the others in my father's halls." He opened his mouth to say something further, then turned to her instead. "That's no way to live, is it?"

"I guess not."

The two shared a smile, then headed into the sun.

In perhaps the most frightening thing to happen yet, the vampire had attempted to make breakfast. He'd done this by pouring a handful of porridge into a pot, then setting that pot on the fire. He'd been personally offended when it started to smoke, then worried. What was he missing?

"It needs some water." Eden came up behind him, pressing a kiss to his cheek. "I'll get some. The rest of you can start with the fruit."

Only then did Kiera notice the assortment laid out beside the fire. There were apples and pears. Wild strawberries and some of the grapes they'd found by the trail a day before. Hidden near the back, there were even a few nectarines, though where they had come from was anyone's guess.

"This looks amazing," she murmured, staring at the back of Evander's head. She suspected the immortal had something to do with the casual plating. "Thank you for preparing it."

The vampire nodded curtly, then surprised them further. Instead of keeping his distance, as he usually did during mealtimes, he settled at the fire beside them, offering a murmured greeting as the fae's footsteps faded away. Only then were all three of them struck with the sudden conundrum.

...awkward.

By the time it was quiet, it was unbearably quiet. Eden usually brought the laughter, and to have lost him on such a morning. Jesse poked a stick in the dirt. Kiera silently choked on a pear.

Evander looked from one to the other before his lips quirked in a dry smile.

"It was fantastic."

Like clockwork, everyone started talking at once.

"Jess, did you see the strawberries?" Kiera crammed her own mouth full of them so she wouldn't be expected to speak. "They're the same kind we found by the river."

"And these?" Jesse reached for a nectarine with a look of delight. Such treats were seldom seen in the forest. "We were only in the tent for a moment. How did you possibly—"

"Don't," Evander said suddenly, catching his wrist. "He likes those."

Jesse froze in his grip, then let it drop back to the blanket.

When the fae appeared a moment later, he was still frozen in place. The vampire smiled sweetly and made room for him to sit, while the shifter leaned abruptly forward.

"Mind if I have that?" He pointed to the same nectarine that had been taken from him. The one that the vampire had been nudging casually into the fae's line of sight.

Eden hardly glanced up before answering. "Of course not. Help yourself."

Jesse snatched the fruit in triumph, leaning back with a spiteful smile. But it was quick to fade. The longer the vampire stared without expression, the more nervous he seemed to become.

After only a few seconds, he set it back down.

"So are we even going to hike today?" he asked briskly, in a rather transparent attempt to shift attention. "The sun has already crossed its zenith. It will be getting dark before long."

"Of course we are," Eden answered in surprise. "We'll just be leaving a bit later than usual. I have travelled with the two of you long enough, I can't imagine you would complain." He waited for a response with a preemptive smile. When he didn't get one, he turned to the shifter. "We have been scouting all night, Jesse. Scouting on *your* behalf. Would you throw that back in my face?"

Kiera snickered under her breath. Evander reclaimed the nectarine.

"You were scouting so *quietly*," the shifter replied. "I didn't hear a thing."

He smiled along as the others laughed, but the whole exchange was a bit sharper than he'd intended. Perhaps he was remembering those bites strewn across the fae's body. His eyes drifted silently between the two immortals, tightening around the edges, as the others planned for the day.

IT WAS ONE OF THOSE sacred days for travelers. A rare combination of both indulgence and luck. Not only were the friends unable to go very far, it was an incomparably easy journey.

They wandered along at a leisurely pace, somehow avoiding the sharp inclines and harrowing slopes that had plagued them before. The trail they had chosen wound along the sunlit fields instead, across even ground with none of the usual pitfalls to ensnare them. It was too open for predators, although few had ventured near after the vampire's arrival, yet too small to risk encountering the bandits that sometimes plagued the country roads. For once, the friends could simply let their guards down and enjoy the experience. And some of them were determined to do just that.

Kiera watched with a smile as the vampire blurred into a grove of dogwood, reappearing a moment later with a blossom that he pressed into the fae's hand. Eden startled reflexively, his hair blowing from his face, but already he was starting to smile. It had been an adjustment, getting used to the abruptness of Evander. Unlike most people, vampires had no transitional movement. They were at the start, then they were at the finish, seeming almost to appear.

The fae bit off a petal and blew it playfully into his face, chattering all the while. When the vampire murmured something serious in reply, he threw back his head with a burst of laughter.

He looks like a boy. I have never seen him like this.

"If we were hoping to catch something for dinner, it's long since fled," Jesse called loudly, marching up the center of the trail. He alone had seemed untouched by the magic of the day. "I would be happy to flee myself," he added under his breath, "anything to get a little peace and quiet."

Eden glanced over his shoulder in surprise, then doubled back up the trail.

There had been many moments, since the friends had set off on their grand adventure, many moments when the hike became too much, or the hours became too long, or despite the twinkling sunshine, the day seemed to have inexplicably soured. There was little rhyme or reason to it. It was a melancholy that affected each of them alike. To combat its evil forces, the fae had developed a cure.

"Shall I sing to you again?"

Jesse stiffened like someone had stabbed him with a blade. "Eden, I really wish you wouldn't—"

"There was a lovely maiden, with starlight in her eyes, who wept beside a river, for want to be a bride. She went unto the fairies, to ask what could be done. They told her to go fishing, and wed what she had won."

The others snorted with laughter, though Jesse's face remained hard. The fae was prone to such outbursts, he used them as weapons. The trick was to clear one's mind, keep from listening. Of course, that was no easy task with a cheerful immortal serenading one with every step.

"Into that sparkling river, the maiden cast her net. She drew a man so ugly, his face I can't forget."

Kiera laughed again, feeling guilty all the while. Whenever pressed, the fae had claimed they were 'tavern classics,' but she was beginning to suspect he made them up on the spot. They were all new to the vampire. He turned halfway to listen, a little smile curving up his cheek.

"She took him to the fairies, his features to erase."

At that point, Eden removed his arm from the shifter's shoulders and circled around in front. He planted himself there without a hint of shame, singing directly into his friend's face.

"They sprinkled bits of SUNSHINE—"

Jesse cracked with a smile.

"—into the bastard's face."

The others broke into peripheral applause, as Jesse clapped his hands slowly, regarding the fae with a reluctant smile. "You are a monster."

"I am *your* monster," the fae corrected with a grin. "Now are you going to tell me what's troubling you? Or shall I compose a second verse?"

Jesse's eyes flashed to the vampire. "Maybe later."

Subtle.

Evander rolled his eyes, then said loudly, "I'll go check something on the trail." A second later, he'd vanished into the ether.

Eden looked after him with a grin, then turned to Jesse. "What is your problem?"

Instead of answering, the shifter countered with a question of his own. "How can you possibly sleep with him?"

Eden leaned back in surprise. "What?"

The two had grown very comfortable with each other—probably more than either had expected—but there were still lines they would never cross. At least, he'd thought there were lines.

But the young wolf stood his ground.

"How can you possibly be attracted to that man?" he demanded. "He's unsettling, and abrasive, and unapologetically homicidal. He tried to kill you, Eden. Now you sleep with him."

The fae waited for more, then tilted his head. *"Yes."*

A gust of silence fell between them.

"I'm sorry, was there a question in that?"

"Forget it," Jesse muttered, continuing up the path. "You want to risk your life every time the sun goes down, that is your business, not mine. Just be sure to leave that map somewhere Kiera and I can find it—"

Eden paused in the middle of the trail, staring after him.

"You're...protective." It had taken him a moment to find the word, it had surprised him even then. As if that particular emotion was used so often in regards to the others, he could not imagine it applying to himself. His eyes lit with curiosity as they settled on his friend. "Why?"

The shifter flushed and glanced away. "You think I'm being protective, just because I think it's a bad idea for a fae to get involved with a vampire? You don't think I'm...I don't know...*sane*?"

"This is more than that." Eden tilted his head, looking the wolf up and down. "Tell me. Why are you so troubled by this?"

Jesse's face colored and he bit the inside of his lip, looking as though he sincerely regretted bringing it up. At the same time, something in him pushed ahead.

"Why am I troubled by it?" he quoted sarcastically. "Forgive me for having a problem with one of my *best friends* sharing his bed with someone genetically predisposed to end his life."

There was a ringing silence.

"Best friends?" The fae regarded him fondly, eyes twinkling with a smile. "You think we are best friends, you and I?"

Jesse curled his fingers, missing his claws. "I think you are a *monster*. As I have already said."

Their eyes met for a brief moment.

"We are best friends," Eden said plainly, returning to the trail. "I just didn't think you were smart enough to have figured that out."

The shifter stopped in his tracks, glaring at the back of his head, while Kiera flitted up beside him. She slipped her hand into his, squeezing it gently and trying very hard to keep a straight face.

"I hate that guy," he muttered. "With all my heart...I hate him."

She patted him on the shoulder with a smile. "I think he knows that, too."

THE DAYS WERE GETTING longer, slipping into the heart of summer. The world was coming to pieces, fraying at the seams. And the vampire and fae were falling quietly in love in the background.

It had started as little gestures; bringing each other sweet tokens, finding reasons to linger in each other's company, combing fingers through waves of sun-warmed hair. A day after *the immortal reckoning*, as Kiera had taken to calling it, the two had begun the hike in their usual places, with the vampire watching from behind and the fae scouting in front. Gradually, as the day progressed, they began drifting nearer and nearer to the middle, until finally, they found themselves side by side.

Eden lowered a hand silently between them. Evander did the same. Their fingers brushed, then wound together. They had been holding onto one another ever since.

"I don't understand how it happened," Jesse remarked one day, stoking at the fire as the evening sun shone through the trees. "Just on a fundamental level. How did Evander stop from killing him that first day after the festival? The ending of your story...it is more what I'd expect."

Looking at the pair now, it seemed a jest that one would ever try to harm the other.

Eden was lounging with his head in the vampire's lap as Evander stroked idle fingers through his hair. A tune lingered in the air between them, hummed in the fae's quiet voice.

It was the same one the bards had been singing.

Their song, Kiera realized.

"Is it really so strange?" she murmured, already lulled by the gentle popping of the fire. It was easy to speak in private those days; the immortals had eyes only for each other. "One fears the quiet, the other fears the stillness. They both come from a timeless people and both are desperate to make that time matter, desperate to feel." She shrugged. "What greater feeling is there than love?"

Jesse opened his mouth to answer, then looked down at her with a sudden smile. "Sometimes I wonder if you're able to hear yourself, if you know the rarity of such a perspective. Sometimes I wonder if you realize how remarkable it is, the things you say."

She pulled back in surprise, thinking he must be teasing her. "I was being honest—"

"So was I." His eyes sparkled as he pressed an unexpected kiss to her cheek. "It's one of the things I love most about you. You see things for what they are. You see how they are meant to be."

A flush of heat bloomed in her cheeks and she lowered her eyes swiftly, fighting back the urge to smile. He'd been saying things like that more and more since that day in the woods, when he'd shifted to a wolf and knelt before her. She never knew what to say in return.

They eased back into conversation, unaware they were being observed themselves.

"It's like they always forget we can hear them," Eden murmured, tilting his head so waves of hair fell across the vampire's leg. "Speaking about us so brazenly in the open, though Kiera is always sweet about it. It's a level of distraction I truly cannot understand."

Evander smiled faintly, playing absentmindedly with his braids. "He surfaces long enough from a daydream to criticize the attention of others..."

The fae glanced up at him. "What?"

The vampire grinned. His lover was full of contradictions like that. Sharp as an arrow one moment, and blissfully detached the next. Always hearing more than what others might expect, always caring less. And always caring more—far more than anyone he'd ever met.

"You have been watching this play out?" he asked softly. "The two of them?"

"Like a childhood story," the fae answered with a smile. "Truth be told, it's made me feel quite tender towards them. But I've had no one to share it with before now."

By the looks of things, that was unlikely to change. The vampire could not be less interested in the love affairs of mortals, but he was indulgent with the fae. He smiled in return, glancing over.

"Shall we place bets on how long it lasts?"

"Have you any money?" Eden asked in surprise.

Evander shrugged, fingers twisting in his hair. "We could bet other things."

The fae grinned, but moved off the vampire's legs—settling more comfortably upon the ground. Comfortable was a relative term. For the last few nights, the two had been sleeping together outside. Sleeping was also a relative term. But the hour was late and the day's journey had been long.

"Later," he promised drowsily, "and later again. For now, let us sleep."

Evander settled immediately beside him, stretching out his long legs as he gazed up into the night sky. The two had made a habit of doing that together—lying on their backs and pointing their fingers as they traced the constellations one by one. Eden knew the names of them all. He'd been taught by his mother, who'd been taught by her mother. The vampire had never known their names, never heard their stories. His people did not have legends for such things.

Eden shivered beside him, and he glanced over in concern.

"Do you want my cloak? It may get colder tonight."

Those bright eyes opened slowly, blinking at the stars.

"Then tonight, we shall sleep inside." He said it just loudly enough to stop the conversation happening on the other side of the camp. Kiera and Jesse looked over at the same time, meeting his eyes. "If that's all right with everyone...?"

He phrased it as a question, but there was a slight edge to his tone—as though it would only remain a question, as long as no one dared to refuse. They hesitated, then nodded quickly.

"Of course."

"Sure."

We'll just stack on top of each other, I guess.

The fae pushed to his feet with a smile, reaching down a hand to Evander. The vampire was quite a bit less certain—looking almost as nervous as those first few nights he'd spent in the camp.

"Is that a good idea?" he murmured, watching as the others filed inside. "I don't mind sleeping outside, Eden. There is no reason for you to stay—"

The fae kissed him silent, then pulled at his wrist.

BY THE TIME EVANDER made up his mind and lifted the door to the tent, the others had already settled in their usual places. It was a tight squeeze with only two people—it was nearly suffocating with three. Usually it didn't matter, seeing as one of them would always be on watch, but the woods were quiet and the shifter had already run in a wide circle to check the perimeter. Between that and the vampire sleeping so close, there was little need for anything else.

"Not so glamourous, huh?" Kiera teased, twisting her hair into braids.

They had become a requirement from the others, given how many times they'd nearly choked to death on her crimson mane. Some nights, Eden helped her weave them.

"It's nice," Evander stammered, frozen uncertainly in the frame.

Another relative term. In the beginning, the fae had insisted things be kept as tidy as possible, but the others had been a creeping influence, and now, it bore a far greater resemblance to a burrow than a tent. Blanket heaped upon blanket, with no borders or delineations. The friends had begun to simply tunnel somewhere in the middle—fighting for space and warmth.

Eden was already lying on his side, gazing towards the entrance with a particularly tender expression, as if he could feel the vampire's nerves. After a moment, he beckoned with his hand. "Come here."

Evander picked his way carefully through the others and slid down beside him, his back pressed snug against the fae's chest. A rush of panic seized him then, an intense claustrophobia made all the worse by the pooling combination of all those scents. There was no space for him here, he didn't know why it had been such a craving. But no sooner had he settled, than the fae's arms circled around him—anchoring him there with a tender, almost childlike embrace.

A quiet thrill quickened his heartbeat. His lips curved in a dawning smile.

This is new.

He lowered his head slowly, resting it lightly upon the pillowed blankets like the others. He didn't know if he'd ever slept with a pillow. He didn't know if he'd ever slept in someone's arms. It was enough novelty to have a roof over his head, let alone to find himself the company of others.

Eden's eyes closed almost immediately, but Evander kept his wide open.

He wanted to prolong the sensation as much as possible.

He didn't want to fall asleep.

Chapter 10

Apart of Kiera thought it might be terrifying to share a tent with a vampire. It sounded like one of those frightening stories that children told each other around the fire—one intended to teach some kind of lesson, but was really just used to scare. But there was something strangely comforting about it. Perhaps it was the inherent safety that came with him. Perhaps it was the look on his face.

Evander had not slept more than a few passing moments. Every time he started to drift off, his eyes would flicker around the tent once more and warm with a secret smile. He kept himself awake instead, savoring it, drawing out every lingering moment spent in the fae's arms.

Kiera had watched with a secret smile before finally drifting off herself.

"Good morning," she said brightly, pushing the tent open and wandering outside. Jesse and Eden were already deep in conversation beneath the oaks that bordered the campsite. Evander was watching from his usual perch beside the fire. She rubbed her arms, peering up at the thin layer of clouds blanketing the sky. "It's quite a bit colder this morning. I'm glad the two of you slept inside."

The vampire nodded faintly, then threw her a sudden glance.

"Thank you for allowing it to happen," he said softly. "There is much you have allowed," he added abruptly. "I would thank you for that as well."

She looked down in surprise, then settled beside him.

Someone's still feeling warm from the tent.

"It's my pleasure. Truly."

The two leaned back against the rocks, watching the others in companionable silence.

It was one of Kiera's favorite kind of mornings. The kind that was slow to start, with no imminent danger pressing against them. The kind that made her wonder how things might have been if they'd met under different circumstances, without a monstrous dragon roaming the skies.

Whatever the two men were discussing, it had long ceased to be a conversation.

Jesse was talking at the speed of light, making grand gesticulations with his arms, while Eden nodded thoughtfully beside him, chewing an apple and leaning against the base of the tree. A little squirrel had scampered down to investigate, venturing closer and closer, with eyes on the fruit. As the shifter prattled on obliviously, Eden broke off a little piece and offered it between them. Two tiny hands reached out and took it, cramming full its mouth, before vanishing up the tree.

Evander shook his head with a faint smile.

"It is like a gift, that I should have met him," he murmured, almost as though he was speaking to himself. "But I wonder who would have given such a thing."

Kiera flashed him a look, warming with a smile. "Gifts are bestowed upon the worthy," she answered casually. "That's something my mother always used to say." It was a lie. Her mother never said that. "At any rate, you've gotten the wrong measure of him. The fae is a nightmare, we don't know why you like him so much."

To her great surprise, the vampire actually laughed—pushing lightly to his feet and offering a hand for her as well. "Come, we have much ground to cover."

DAYS HAD PASSED SINCE the immortals clashed, then settled in the forest. Blissful, sunlit days, where they made terrible time. They'd been hoping to reach the river country the night before, but it was still lost behind the horizon. Mostly because it had been like trying to wrangle children.

That morning was looking to be more of the same.

"You will frighten it away," Evander called again, shielding his eyes from the sun as the fae swung himself into the highest branches of a tree. "You will only frighten it, Eden."

"I will not frighten it," the fae insisted, easing onto a slender perch. "Things do not run from me the way they do from you." He glanced down at a ridiculously precarious moment, jerking his head to the vampire. "Pure evil, that one. Really lives up to the name."

Jesse chuckled under his breath while Kiera pointed furiously at the ground.

"Get down this instant! You will break open your head!"

"Is that Mother calling?" Eden replied innocently, vanishing a moment behind a cloud of leaves. "Tell her to speak up."

The vampire rolled his eyes impatiently. "Just *leave* it, I will not even care."

But the fae had no intention of leaving anything. He lingered a moment longer, hovering just outside their line of sight, then leapt triumphantly to the ground. "There—I've got it!"

The friends gathered round, staring with a mix of expressions.

"You weren't kidding," Jesse finally managed. "You were looking for a butterfly."

The tiny creature was perched upon his finger, its delicate body shielded by the curve of his hand. He stroked it absentmindedly, playing with the tips of its wings.

"Yes, what did you think I meant?"

"I'd hoped it was metaphorical."

The fae ignored this, holding it proudly to the vampire.

"There—you see? The beach I was telling you about. It is *exactly* that color blue." His eyes danced with excitement, along with a touch of pride. "I told you...things do not run."

His friends stared back in silence.

It was in these moments Kiera wondered if the fae realized how strange he appeared to the rest of the world, how very different he was from everything around him. Perhaps all of the fair folk were the same, perhaps her eyes had muddied with mortality. Or perhaps the vampire was right.

Perhaps he was a gift.

"You are *insane*, Eden." Jesse clapped him on the shoulder—inadvertently frightening the butterfly away. "When this is over, we are taking you to see a healer. Surely something can be done."

The fae stared after it in dismay before turning back to Evander. "Did you see?" he asked hopefully. "Did you see before it flew away?"

A look of pure tenderness lit the vampire's eyes, gone in a flash. "Here's a surprise—I don't care."

Kiera snorted with laughter, heading back up the trail.

She was surprised by how sharp they were with each other, and surprised by how sweet. A few days before, the fae had whittled the vampire a muzzle, then kissed him all over the face.

Eden fell into step alongside him, muttering under his breath. "You cared a *little*."

The vampire shot him a sideways glance, lips twitching with a smile.

A few seconds passed, then without even a trace of warning, he leapt straight vertical like a cat, coming down in a wild pounce atop the fae's unsuspecting head.

"Wait—"

Eden's voice cut off in a burst of laughter as the pair tussled around like cubs, rolling in violent spirals across the forest floor. Flashes of bright hair spun together, in a mix of shouts and little snarls. There were several points of sharp impact, until the fae detached himself suddenly and came up with a blade—holding it threateningly to the vampire's neck.

"Behave, or I will make you."

Evander gazed up at him, dark eyes catching the light. With a little smile, he trailed his fingers slowly up the length of the blade, keeping his eyes on the fae the whole time. "Go on then...*make* me."

A deep blush warmed the fae's skin, striking like flint in his eyes. Kiera was half-convinced he was going to jump on the vampire right then. He didn't. He just lowered the blade with a smile.

And such a smile it was. Kiera had never seen one like it.

The cougar came out of nowhere.

It was much harder to predict things when they do not behave as one might expect. It was why they didn't see the creature coming. It had approached from the wrong direction.

It had selected Evander as its prey.

There was a sharp intake of breath as the friends looked at the last second—all of them looking too late. Evander was still frozen on the ground in surprise. Eden was still turning.

"No!"

A blistering snarl tore through the air as Eden caught the beast with his bare hand—caught it by the jaw. Those lethal fangs sank deep into his palm and he let out an involuntary cry, bracing all his weight against it. He pushed it away from the vampire, using nothing but the strength of a single arm, but Evander had already risen and grabbed hold of it—snapping the creature's neck.

It fell with a *thud* on the ground beside them, its claws still reaching forward, its fangs still dripping with immortal blood.

"Are you mad?!" Evander cried, rounding upon the fae. He reached automatically to steady him, but his face was white with rage. "I could have stopped it!"

"I did not want you to try," Eden panted, rigid with pain. "What if you had missed?"

Jesse took a step forward, still shaken by the sight.

"Why did it jump at you in the first place?" he murmured, kneeling to examine it. Normally, he wouldn't get so close, but the beast was clearly dead. "We have these cats in the woods where I grew up. They're cautious for their size. They would never..."

His face whitened, as he fell abruptly silent.

"What's wrong?" Kiera asked, pushing forward. "What is it?"

She froze a second later, staring at the cloud of foam slowly frothing from the creature's mouth. Those cats had roamed the woods around Cattling as well, she knew just what it meant. It was why they were taught to flee such things as children. It was a sentence good as death.

It was madness.

"What is it?" Evander asked over his shoulder, still examining the shredded strips of the fae's hand. "Is there another?" When no one answered, he turned to check for himself.

He saw the foam, and his face went still.

"Eden," he said softly, "the beast was sick."

Kiera would think back on that moment many times in the days to come, wondering why he didn't choose to shield him, wondering why he told the fae the second he knew. Each of her own instincts had risen in sharply the other direction. But it was already over, the damage was done.

Eden turned a bit unsteadily, eyes tracing over the cougar's mouth. He dulled for a moment, as if he'd grown suddenly tired, before his face tightened with a searing flash of pain.

"I would cut it off, but it's too deep. It will have already spread."

Kiera blinked at him slowly, realizing a second too late that he was talking about his own hand. Her eyes drifted towards it in a daze, as if some part of her was waiting to wake up. He was right about the damage. The skin was in ribbons. In some places, she could see bone.

His forehead fell limp against the vampire's shoulder.

"It stings..."

Evander picked him up at once, leaping over the carcass and racing straight back the way they'd come. He did this at a vampire's speed, giving no thought as to the people he was leaving behind him. They threw each other a quick look, then did the only thing in their power.

They started to run.

THERE WAS NO MATCHING a vampire for speed, but Eden had blacked out twice from the pain, and Evander had stopped immediately to revive him. By the time the others raced back to their old camp, the immortals were just reaching it themselves, blurring out of nowhere to a sudden stop.

"Pitch the tent," Evander instructed without looking, "and boil some water." He pointed blindly from one person to the next. "You—patrol the woods, look for anything else that is acting strange." He glanced up suddenly, catching the shifter's eye. "Jesse...do not let anything bite you."

Jesse nodded shakily, then threw off his clothes—shimmering into a wolf before the last of the pieces had finished falling, and entering the woods at a run.

"Speak to me," Evander lowered the fae gently to the ground, cupping a hand around his cheek, "let me know you're there."

Eden blinked up at him, half-dazed by the pain. "...you didn't appreciate my butterfly."

The vampire's eyes tightened and he threw a look over his shoulder. "Where is the water?!"

Kiera raced back and forth across the clearing, balancing armfuls of wood. They tumbled into a haphazard pile, knocking against each other as she scrambled to find something to light.

"You only said it a moment ago, I'm still making a fire—"

"Forget the water," Eden said weakly, hitching up on his arms. "And stop acting like I'm doomed already, there is something yet to try." He turned to Evander, his eyes growing heavy in the blinding sun. "There is a flower my people use for such things. Can you find some for me?"

The vampire nodded at once, gripping his uninjured hand. "What is it called?"

The fae wavered as the image lurched dizzily before him.

"I'm not..." He squinted his eyes, working hard to draw a breath. "I can't remember. I can't remember what we're talking about."

Kiera froze dead still behind him. Evander's grip tightened on his hand.

"Eden," his voice was soft, drawing him back again, "what's the name of the flower?"

The fae's eyes opened wider, like part of him had been asleep. "It is...I only know the name in the old tongue. Hyacinth. They call it something different now."

Evander nodded again, already pushing to his feet. "Remthorne. I will get some." He threw a glance back at Kiera. "You will stay with him?"

She hurried forward, sinking to her knees. "Of course. Every second."

The vampire opened his mouth, like he wanted to say something more. Then he was gone in a rush of wind, just a streak of shadow vanishing into the trees.

The fae and the barmaid shared a fleeting look.

Then they settled down to wait.

TIME PASSED SLOWLY, like a creeping chill.

For endless hours it seemed, Kiera gazed down upon the fae—murmuring little comforts, smoothing strands of damp hair away from his face. He was burning, unlike anything she'd ever felt before. While the pain in his hand must have been extraordinary, he hardly seemed to notice. His eyes were over-bright and dilated—gazing at times without seeing, into the open sky.

After a long while, he spoke.

"This madness," he said hoarsely, a far cry from his usual voice, "have you seen it?"

She nodded stiffly.

"When I was a child, a woman in our village was bitten by a fox in a similar state. She'd thought it was hurt and needed tending, she offered out her hand." He tried to swallow, but his mouth was dry.

"What happened to her?"

There was a pause, followed by a hasty look. "She died."

So why the HELL did I tell that story?

She threw him another look, desperate to reassure him, even more desperate to cool him down. She wished for the hundredth time that she'd gotten water from the river before Evander had left. It was so close that she could hear it, but a part of her was terrified to leave the fae alone.

"She was old," she stammered apologetically. "It isn't...it isn't the same."

The fae nodded faintly, but he'd already made up his mind.

"The map is in my bag," he said quietly, "keep my bow and send word to my father. Any of my kin can find him." He drew in a ragged breath, getting a little less air each time. "Evander will stay with you—you may count on that. He'll help you and Jesse see this through."

She shook her head slowly, unable to believe they were discussing it. That cheerful sun bore down like a hammer upon them—stunning her senses and stealing her breath.

But the fae was not finished. There was more.

"Keira...you will do something for me?" His eyes locked with hers—tinged with red, but still the clearest blue. "I may live, I may not. But there is no in between." He paused a split second, drawing in a deep breath. "If I begin to lose hold on myself...you must promise to end it."

She fell utterly silent, feeling as though time itself had lurched to a stop. A lone cougar, out on the prowl. A rushed conversation by the ferns? This *could not* be happening.

But the fae had never been so sincere.

"You must promise me," he said again. "Quickly, before the others get back."

She leaned abruptly closer, emphasizing every word.

"This *is not happening*. Blisserin and Carpathians, wolf packs and trolls. A thousand terrors you have survived, Eden. This is *not* what gets to claim you."

He tried to speak, but she beat him to it. It was easy to beat him.

That alone made it feel as though she couldn't breathe.

"The flowers will work. They *have* to work," she said it with certainty, though she felt absolutely none. Never had her people known of any cure. "You just need to stay here, alright? We can fix this. We're going to fix this." She was crying now. "An hour ago, you were fine."

He smiled sadly. Still lovely, even near the end.

"But that is the way these things go. And I do not wish...I do not wish to remain in such a state." He shivered as the fever tore through him, imagining the worst. "Myself, but not myself. A stranger in my own mind. You must not let that happen to me. You must take a knife—"

"Eden, it will *never* come to that."

"You must take a knife and end it." He took a blade from his belt and slapped it into her hand, guiding her wrist until the point was pressed to a specific place on his neck. "Right here, do you understand? One quick slice and I will bleed out in seconds."

She sobbed quietly, pulling away. "*Please* stop—"

"Jesse won't have the heart, and Evander will stop you if you try." He reached for her hand, panting with the effort. "You are the only person I can ask. Please...for me."

Evander would rip me to pieces. Jesse would set those pieces on fire.

And I...would let them.

Her head was spinning, and the blade was heavy in her palm. So heavy, she felt like it would drag her straight into the ground. Another tear slipped down her face, but a finger lifted her chin.

"Kiera...*madness?*" His eyes were shining. He shook his head. "You must promise."

Their eyes met and she let out a breath.

"I promise."

The knife slipped into her belt and she turned deliberately to other things—cupping her cool fingers across his scorching brow.

"It makes no difference," she repeated lightly, "we're going to fix this. Evander is finding those flowers and the fever will burn itself away. I'm telling you...everything will be fine."

They shared a lingering look, then he nodded quickly.

"Yes, I'm sure it will be fine."

The sun began to slide across the mountains, casting slanted shadows from the sky. Kiera dragged the fae into the shade, laying his head gently in her lap. Her fingers combed rhythmically though his damp hair, while she hummed a tune under her breath. It was something she hadn't thought of since childhood. She had no idea what had suddenly made her think of it again.

"Is he alive?!"

There was a gust of wind, then Evander was kneeling beside them, a crop of brightly-colored flowers clutched in his fist. Judging by the tears in his clothing, he must have flown across the entire mountain range. Judging by the look on his face, he hadn't flown quickly enough.

"He is asleep," she breathed. "I can no longer wake him."

There was a shifting on her legs.

"I'm not asleep," the fae murmured, gazing slowly up at them, "I was listening." His eyes took a moment to focus, settling on her face. "That was a lovely song."

The blossoms appeared in front of him, just inches from his eyes.

"Is this enough?" Evander panted. "There weren't many. I grabbed everything I could."

Eden coughed weakly, nodding at the same time. "Those are perfect. I will tell you what to do."

The vampire settled hastily before him, throwing Kiera a swift look. "Leave."

She nodded and pushed shakily her feet, stumbling backward as the vampire began ripping the petals apart. Eden watched for a moment, then caught her eye over his shoulder.

"Do not go far."

She nodded again, teeth digging into her lip.

The trees closed up in front of her. A second later, she was gone.

THE FAE WAS UP ALL night with a fever, tossing and turning inside the tent. Evander stayed by his side while the others lingered in the clearing—listening to the night birds, staring at the fire.

Kiera was sitting on the ground, holding the fae's bow.

All night long, his words had played back through her mind—each one boring inside a little deeper. They flared up with a dull ache as she touched over them, like skin closed over a thorn.

If I begin to lose hold on myself...you must promise to end it.

Right here, do you understand? One quick slice and I will bleed out in seconds.

Please...for me.

He'd left her his bow. Send word to his father, but keep the bow. She trailed her fingers over the wood, finding the same grooves where his fingers had held for hundreds of years. She could not imagine a day when someone else would carry it. When it wouldn't be safe in his hand.

Could I really kill him?

The dagger pressed hard against her leg.

"They are quiet now," Jesse murmured, settling wearily beside her. The woods had been empty and he'd been staring at the fire for hours. "I cannot hear them murmuring as before."

Her eyes drifted to the tent, unsure whether that was good or bad.

A part of her wanted to tell him. To share the burden, get an outside perspective. But Eden had been right about the shifter. He could not bring himself to do such a thing, any more than he could allow it. After the death of his brother, life held a different precedence than it did before.

She didn't tell him. She pulled out her stone instead.

"Did I ever show you this?"

He glanced over, then reached a curious hand. "No, what is it?"

"Just a trinket," she answered, dropping it in his palm. "Marrow gave it to me, for *luck*."

She couldn't help but place a sour emphasis on the word. His green eyes flashed to hers for a moment before he raised it to the light. "It's pretty." He angled it back and forth before tossing it back into her hands. "That was sweet of him, I guess. If he couldn't give us answers..."

She traced the edges. It had been flushed beneath her fingers, but returned cold as ice.

"Would you like me to put another log on the fire?" she offered, eyeing him with a trace of concern. "You must be freezing—"

"*Kiera!*"

Her heart stopped as her eyes shot to the tent. For a split second, she couldn't bear to see what might be inside. But she scrambled to her feet, racing forward.

"I'm coming—"

The door pulled back, and she slid to a stop.

Eden smiled. "You look *terrible*."

She let out a breath of laughter, then another. Then she covered her mouth, holding back a tired sob. Jesse wandered up carefully behind her, letting out a quiet sigh of relief.

"The fever has broken." Evander turned to them with a glowing smile, looking like someone had brought him back from the grave. "The danger has passed."

"As I said it would." Eden shook with a cough, pushing higher onto the bed. "My people are blessed with a godlike resilience. There was never any need for alarm."

The vampire reached over swiftly to help him.

"Evan, I am fine."

Evan?

Evander helped him anyway, propping him against the pillows, before pushing abruptly to his feet. "I'm going to get more flowers in case the fever comes back. He will need more water as well—though he doesn't like to drink it." The men shared a hard look. "You must persuade him."

Unsurprisingly, Jesse volunteered to fetch the water.

"You will be here when I return?" the vampire asked, squeezing the fae's hand.

It was the same question he'd asked each morning when they'd first begun travelling together, terrified his new companions would flee each time he left to hunt.

Eden gazed up with a tender smile. "Where else would I go?"

The vampire kissed him swiftly, a hand cupped around his head, then vanished swiftly out the door—but not before leaving his beloved with a parting threat.

"Let me be perfectly clear...you may never die," he said bluntly. "I forbid it. There will never be a good enough reason, there will never be a worthy enough cause. And if you should ever decide to try," he continued, pacing back across the tent, "if you get any more clever ideas in that pretty little head...I will hunt you to the ends of the earth. And I will kill you again myself."

They locked eyes, then the vampire kissed him again.

"Drink your water."

He was gone a moment later, leaving a chilling silence in his wake.

Kiera stared after him, not at all surprised to discover her feet had locked to the ground. She took a second to detach them, then settled herself beside the fae.

"...not sweet."

The tension vanished as both remembered their conversation outside Farion. She had wondered as to his lack of attraction. He had claimed to have a certain type.

Eden laughed softly, then his face grew still. "He is, actually." His eyes lifted to hers. "Is that strange?"

She considered a moment. "It's just people, right?"

He smiled again, nodding. "It's just people."

They sat there quietly for a while—thinking of where the day had started, thinking of where it had ended up. After a few seconds of silence, he lifted his gaze.

"Did you bring it?"

She opened her cloak to show the dagger underneath.

A peculiar expression stole across his features—something like anticipation, something like grief. In the end, he was merely grateful.

"Thank you."

She nodded and slipped beneath his arm. The blade passed between them, sheathing itself safe in the fae's belt. She tried not to think of it. She tried not to think of anything.

A few more seconds passed, and she started to cry.

Chapter 11

The fae slept through the next day, through the next night, and late again into the next morning. His friends took advantage of the opportunity to gather supplies.

There wasn't much coin left after their series of misadventures, but there was plenty that could be traded the next time they found themselves in a town. The river people were said to make their living primarily through bargaining with outsiders. They would have such fundamentals as shelter and food, but they might be lacking in certain things found higher in the mountains.

Walnuts and mushrooms were stuffed deep into satchels. Honey and fresh juices were stored in the empty flasks. There was apparently an expensive oil that could be made by pressing the leaves of a certain alpine flower, though for the life of her, Kiera couldn't manage it—but she was able to find a grove of red sander which was nearly as pricey, valued for its vibrant color in dyes.

By the time they returned to camp, Eden had strayed from the tent and was highly offended to have found himself deserted in his hour of need. He was proceeding to make this well known.

"I'd like to personally thank whoever decided to put the bandages at the very bottom of a pack," he snapped. "Searching for it has been a great therapy for my *recently mangled hand.*"

The rest of them kept their eyes wisely on their own tasks, knowing better by now than to engage. It had been another wise idea to confiscate the fae's weapons before he'd awoken.

"No, don't bother helping," he continued irritably. "I'll get it myself."

He let out a deafening sigh, cradling his injured hand safe against his chest, while the other rifled through the satchel. There was a clumsiness to each movement that hadn't been there before the fever. When his finger caught upon the handle, the whole thing tumbled into the flames.

"The pack is in the fire now," he updated them casually. "Jesse, I believe it was yours."

Kiera watched as the shifter hurried forward, grabbing the handle and scooping it away from the coals. His own hand ached desperately for a blade, but he flashed the fae a saccharine smile instead—sweeping the ash from his belongings and relocating into the nearby trees.

Smart.

The fae sulked a moment at the lack of opposition, then continued to search for something to trim the gauze. When he failed to find anything, he proceeded to loudly demand his blades.

She slipped to the other side of the vampire, careful not to present herself as a target.

"Oh, this is going to be delightful..."

"What do you expect?" Evander answered shortly. "He's fae. They're dramatic, impulsive, and hot-tempered. There can be no reasoning with one in a time like this."

She nodded slowly, flashing a secret smile. "Dramatic, impulsive and hot-tempered...? Not like vampires. The vampires I know aren't like that at all."

He looked at her in surprise. "Are you teasing me, Kiera?"

She froze, suddenly panicked. "...would that be so terrible?"

He stared a second longer before returning to his task. "I'm just amazed you think that's a good idea."

They continued working in silence—one passing over tiny slices of lemon, as the other squeezed them slowly into a jar. It was a thankless task, but one that kept them clear of the fray.

It also permitted them to watch.

Eden could make all the snappish jokes he wanted, but Kiera truly didn't know why he didn't spend every second screaming, given the state of his hand. The bones had been reset, but the lean muscles and delicate tendons were still torn straight through the middle. When the fae had tried to fit an arrow to his bow the day before, he'd doubled over in excruciating pain.

She watched him for a moment, then cast Evander a tentative look.

"I've heard the blood of vampires has healing properties."

For weeks now, she'd wanted to ask him directly. It was nothing but idle gossip, things she'd picked up from travelers passing through the tavern, but like most such things, there was often a shred of truth at the core. And if something like *that* were true...it raised several more questions.

He glanced down at her with a touch of surprise, then returned his eyes to the fae.

"My blood cannot heal him," he murmured quietly as if he'd wished that it could many times before. "We are too different, he and I."

She studied him curiously, surprised by his tone. "You don't seem so different to me."

The ghost of a smile flitted across his face, vanishing just as fast.

"That is because you are young," he answered, his knife curving the peel off the fruit. "If you had been alive as long as I have..." He trailed away. "I wish very much it were true."

They passed the lemons between them, working into an easy rhythm. One cut and the other crushed, over and over, as the little jar slowly filled to the top. It was sour now, that was how it would travel. But soon, the people who traded for it would sweeten the bitterness away.

She replayed his last words, unable to let it rest.

"I don't understand that," she finally murmured. "You claim to be so different, yet Eden cares for you all the same—"

"And that surprises you?" the vampire asked sharply, turning to face her. "Why, because he is better than me? Because I cannot have something so good?"

She lowered her hands in surprise. "Is that what he says?"

There was a pause.

"No," the vampire admitted. "He says exactly the opposite."

Another pause, doubtful this time.

"He says we are the same," Evander clarified, speaking in a sudden rush, each word chasing after the next. "He says the past has little bearing on the present. And that—"

He quieted suddenly, staring into the fire.

"He says a great many things."

ANOTHER DAY PASSED, and the friends continued hiking. Albeit at a slower pace.

At least, that was the intent.

"Could you just walk like a normal person?" Evander chided for the tenth time. "You are making everyone nervous. Could you just *walk* upon the trail?"

Eden swept past with a radiant smile, pressing a loud kiss to his cheek.

The extra day's rest had done wonders, and the fae was starting to feel very much like his old self—restless, and charismatic, and playful as all hell. He had been expressing this like a child with three days of pent-up energy. He had also decided to take the vampire's warnings as a challenge.

"Slow down," Evander repeated fiercely. "Or I will force you."

"Best of luck with that," Jesse remarked, watching as the fae vanished up ahead before reappearing a moment later with a clutch of blackberries in his hand. He popped two into his mouth, then gave the rest to Kiera. "We've tried for months, and never had any luck."

The vampire ground his jaw in frustration. "You do not have fangs."

There was beat of silence.

"...that's a good point."

Their hair blew forward as the fae doubled back again—thinking he might have dropped something, before shifting momentum and shooting back up the trail. Evander's hand flew out to catch him, but even he was not fast enough. He glowered instead, staring in exasperation.

"Stop bounding ahead like that! You were poisoned. You must rest."

Eden froze abruptly, turning on a dime.

"You were poisoned. You must rest."

The others stopped as well, choking down laughter, as he slipped into a frightfully accurate impression of the vampire's voice. He was mimicking him as well, arms folded with a little scowl.

Evander was stunned, having never seen such a thing.

"What are you doing?"

"What are you doing?"

He unfolded his arms.

"This is foolishness, Eden. I haven't time for games."

"I haven't time for games."

Evander nodded slowly, eyes narrowing with a rather frightening expression. Eden turned even more slowly to glance behind him. Seeing nothing, he lifted a hand to his chest in surprise.

Me?

The vampire stood there a second longer, then shot forward like an arrow and tackled the fae around the waist. It might have been terrifying, if Eden weren't laughing uncontrollably all the while. That being said, it still carried a few of those harrowing qualities, particularly when the vampire grew tired of tumbling and simply pinned him violently to the ground.

"Alright, alright," the fae surrendered with a breathless grin. "I'll take this more seriously." He dropped his head to the ground, suddenly dizzy. "...I'll take this more seriously."

Evander studied him with concern. "You need to rest. We should not have left so soon."

The fae studied him in return, tracing a finger along the shadows beneath his eyes. "And you need to hunt." He turned his head to the side, exposing his neck. "Take some from me."

The vampire only smiled, smoothing back his hair.

"You must gather your strength," he replied. "You have none to spare for me. And besides, you are likely still touched with madness. It would explain a great deal." He leaned back on his heels. "But I will hunt."

It was difficult to be around the fae in the best of circumstances. It had been significantly harder when parts of him were constantly soaked in blood.

"Could we stop here for the night?" he asked the others, gesturing to a break in the trees just a little ways off the trail. "The three of you could eat something as well."

They hadn't been walking very long, it was just after mid-day. But there was a good chance the vampire was right about Eden pushing things too quickly. He'd yet to rise from the ground.

"Yes, that's fine." Jesse swung the pack off his shoulder, glancing around for the best place to pitch the tent. It had become somewhat of a transient ritual, a temporary hoisting of a flag, before moving somewhere new. "We've used so many flasks, I need to refill our water anyway."

He cut a line westward before he'd even finished speaking—hearing the distant splash of a river while the girl standing beside him could not. She took his pack instead, grabbing it from his arm, before dragging out the heavy canvas and maneuvering it between two trees. Evander started a fire with a few quick sweeps of his hand. Eden was already sitting beside it.

We are getting good at this. Much better than we were before.

"Wait a moment," the fae spoke up suddenly, playing the words in his mind. "You cannot hunt in these parts. What if other animals are sick? Those flowers would not heal you the same."

The vampire gave him a habitual kiss on the forehead, setting off anyway. "I'll be fine. I can read the signs—"

"No, he's right," Kiera interrupted, heaving the last of the poles into place. "The beast that attacked before was already close to the end, it was obvious. But many others could be infected with the same thing and you would never know it. He's right, Evander. We should get farther away."

The vampire hovered impatiently at the edge of the clearing. "What, then?"

"Just—"

"No, I cannot drink from you," he repeated, as the fae beckoned him closer. "You are in no condition. And I must *hunt*, Eden. It has been too long already."

He considered a moment, then let out a sigh.

"It will have to be from one of them."

Kiera nodded along, then went very still.

Wait...what?

The vampire was already moving towards her, freezing the blood in her veins.

A reflexive cry rose up in her throat, but she could give no air to it. Was such a thing even permitted? He was *the vampire* no longer. He was Evander, her companion. Possibly even her friend.

Were screams no longer an option? Must she indulge him now instead?

A figure appeared between them. Eden had risen swiftly from the fire.

"That will not happen," he said firmly.

Evander paused in surprise. "But you said—"

"I said you should not drink from the animals of the forest, as they could still be touched with madness. I said that if you wish, you are welcome to drink from me. Kiera is *not* an option."

His eyes said a great deal more.

Back. Off.

Not since those first days, had there been such open hostility between them. The vampire didn't know what to make of it now. But he chose a troublesome path.

"You know it will do no lasting harm. I need *blood*, Eden."

"You need to *wait*," the fae countered, looking abruptly tired. "The answer is not that you frighten and take from a defenseless girl. If you will not drink from me, then wait."

The vampire considered a moment, then shook his head. "You are not thinking clearly—"

He took a step forward, shocked again when the fae stood in his way.

"What is this?" he challenged, eyes flashing. "You would send me away?"

Eden stepped right in front of him, staring into his face.

"I'll *stop* you, Evander."

He was utterly expressionless. Utterly calm. That playful boy from the woods had vanished, replaced with the immortal warrior who'd defended her since the day they left Farion.

A thousand snarling terrors had tested him. Not a single one had found a path.

The vampire wasn't angry, as she might have expected. He couldn't seem to get past the surprise. Twice, his eyes flickered towards Kiera—tightening around the edges, as though struck with a problem he'd never considered before. When they returned the fae, the answer was clear.

"I'm sorry," he said abruptly, looking past Eden to the girl cowering behind. "I did not mean to frighten you, or...or take what is not mine. I am just thirsty."

"And I am a person," she answered softly, still rattled beyond belief.

He nodded slowly, not quite following. "That's very convenient. That's what I eat."

Eden's hand twitched towards his blade, but she caught his wrist—stepping carefully around him until she and Evander were standing face to face. Oddly enough, it was the vampire's confusion that had steadied her. There was no animosity, no malice. It had simply never occurred to him *not* to bite her. They were venturing into uncharted territory. Everything was brand new.

"If we were friendly with another vampire," she began quietly, "if we let him come into our camp...would you let him feed upon Eden?"

Evander hissed involuntarily. "Absolutely not. He is mine."

The fae glanced up sharply behind her, not exactly pleased with the vernacular, but he kept his silence. He even allowed her to take a step closer, in reach of the vampire's quick hands.

"But we're all friends," she countered, "we all share. A fae is a vampire's food, just as much as any mortal. Probably even more. What would be so wrong in it?"

A muscle twitched in Evander's jaw. "They wouldn't be able to stop. I don't wish to speak of it—"

"What if they *could* stop?" she pressed gently, staring up at him. "What if they could stop, but they never asked his permission? What if they just grabbed him and fed?" She paused, letting the visual take hold. "Perhaps Eden would have to patrol that night, or hike the next day for many hours. Perhaps we'd be attacked, and he'd be too tired to fight. Perhaps he simply didn't wish it."

She paused again, staring into the vampire's eyes.

"Would it seem convenient to you then?"

The two regarded each other in a charged silence—one that wasn't exactly antagonistic, but there was something pressing about it at the same time. As long as she lived, she'd never be able to interpret the vampire's expression. Those dark eyes were overwhelming, brimming with such feeling that it seemed to spill right out of him and consume them both. If that silence had lasted any longer, she might have asked him what it was. But she never got the chance.

There was a rustling in the trees, then Jesse appeared beside them.

"You must come," he said breathlessly. "I've found the people we're looking for."

Chapter 12

The 'river people,' as Kiera had heard them repeatedly described, were nothing like what she'd come to expect. To start, they didn't live by a river. The friends had passed by one on the way down the slopes, according to Eden, they'd passed several. But the village itself, was just a village.

"I don't understand," she whispered, as they ventured onto a bluff. "Where is all the water?"

Jesse threw her a quick smile, then hoisted her onto his shoulders.

Seven hells!

Her eyes lit up and she let out a gasp of surprise—staring in open-mouthed wonder at the tangle of sunlit ribbons stretching out towards the sky. There were so many, there couldn't possibly be names for all of them. Some were wider than others. Some were choppy, some calm. All of them reminded her of something, a vague image in the periphery, she couldn't quite place what it was.

"It's like veins," she blurted suddenly. "They lace the valley like veins."

The shifter nodded, his dark hair brushing her legs.

"And the village is right at the heart. There are several," he continued, striding alongside the others, as they left the trees and ventured onto the grassy plains, "but from what I've been told, the largest is at the center. People travel between the others by boat, looking for things to trade."

He shot a confirmatory glance at Eden—who nodded in agreement.

"It's a sprawling place, with sprawling people." The fae lifted a hand to shield his eyes from the setting sun. "The perfect spot to travel unnoticed, should one ever wish to hide."

It was easy to believe it. Amidst the tangle of rivers, each one pep-pered with little hamlets, it was easy to imagine how someone could get lost and never return. It wasn't until the others had already started moving, that Kiera understood the silent warning in his words.

He's worried for Jesse. He's worried he might be found.

"The river people are descended from men," he continued lightly, "but there are several packs in the area as well. Might any of them have a connection to yours?"

Jesse stiffened beneath her, rigid as a blade.

"We're too far away," he replied, without much conviction. When the others looked at him, he shrugged it off with a casual smile. "It will be fine, trust me."

Kiera hopped back to the ground, giving his shoulders a quick squeeze. Not for the first time, she wondered if Eden had told the shifter's secret to Evander. Probably. The two were always talking. And while it wasn't in the fae's character to break a confidence, the fact that their fellowship had been casually avoiding the vengeance of a wolf pack, wasn't the kind of thing to keep to oneself.

"Come then," Eden said softly, "the sun is setting. We must find a place to stay the night."

IT DIDN'T TAKE LONG to reach the central hub amidst the web of rivers. The trails were flat and well-worn, thick with the scent of pa-pyrus rustling in the breeze.

"Oh look," Evander said with an ironic smile, "there's so much hy-acinth."

The vampire had run himself ragged, trying to collect enough to fight the fever gripping the fae. Only a few blossoms it had yielded, and he'd run straight through his shoes.

Jesse flashed a teasing grin. "Should have gone this way, I guess."

The vampire lifted his eyebrows. "Are those wolves behind you?"

The shifter tensed in spite of himself, casting a reflexive look over his shoulder. By the time he glanced back, Evander was staring with a wry smile.

"My mistake. Just some dogs."

Well...that settles that.

Eden rolled his eyes, pushing between them to continue down the trail. He made sure to knock into Evander's shoulder as he walked past. "Play nice with the children."

The vampire shrugged stiffly. "He started it."

The village itself was much the same as any other. There was a school and a blacksmith, a butcher and baker, apothecaries and taverns. The houses were a bit smaller, set farther into the reeds. Along one side ran a great forest, while the other opened onto the water. So wide and expansive it had looked from the mountains. So perfectly ordinary it was from the valley floor.

"We can sell off what we've gathered, then meet back at one of the taverns." Eden pointed to a small pub in the distance, one of the few that wasn't on the main road. "How about there?"

The friends agreed and quickly divvied up the supplies between them, each of them setting off in a different direction in search of the best price. For once, there wasn't any need for worry or safety in numbers. As long as they stayed in the village, almost everything was within sight.

Kiera sold the honey they'd collected for three silver pieces. It would probably have brought much less, but she'd chosen her victim carefully and charmed him with a smile. She returned to the others in triumph, thinking hers would be the greatest achievement, only for the fae to beat her. The vampire arrived only a moment after, opening his hand with double what the others had brought.

"That's impossible," Jesse exclaimed, balking in astonishment at the gold twinkling in his palm. "Weren't you bartering for the flint? That was the cheapest thing we had."

"I thought we might use the flint," Evander answered casually. "I didn't sell it."

The others froze at the same time, unwilling to ask the question. After a few seconds, they shoved Kiera forward as sacrifice, elbowing her at the same time.

"Then...where did you get the gold?"

The vampire glanced up in surprise, having thought the conversation already finished. "Oh—I asked for it."

There was a beat of silence. Followed by three matching smiles.

Of course you did.

If a vampire asks for money, you can be damn sure he'll come back with gold.

They headed towards the tavern without a backward glance, clapping Evander on the shoulder as they passed. He looking between them in confusion, before holding up the gold.

"...was that wrong?"

NEEDLESS TO SAY, THE friends had more than enough coin for the tavern. Still, they were cautious with their spending, having learned their lesson before. They paid for a single room on the upper story and settled inside with their sparse belongings. A small bed was set in the corner. The window opened onto a tiny balcony, from which they could see the main road.

"It feels strange to be inside after so long," Kiera murmured, perching on the edge of the mattress. The floorboards were deafening under her boots, while the blankets seemed abnormally soft. She smoothed them slowly beneath her fingers. "We'll have to fight it out for this."

Eden glanced across the room with a grin. "I think Evander has earned it, don't you? Seeing as he could probably buy the village several times over?"

The others chuckled, but the vampire looked thoughtfully towards the bed.

"I've never slept in a bed before," he murmured, "not that I can remember. Perhaps only once. I was hunting and came across an old couple near Vale. There was one in their house."

In hindsight, it was entirely possible he didn't realize the weight of what he was saying. Such things were natural to a vampire, the same as the confrontation in the woods a few hours before. And, it was entirely possible he would *never* had known, but his eyes flashed up when the fae stiffened.

"Do you not wish me to tell you such things?" he asked quietly.

Eden drew in a breath, then continued unpacking. "I wish you to tell me everything."

It might have been true or merely a way to avoid the conversation, but the fae was suddenly in a hurry to leave the room. He abandoned the packs and swept almost immediately for the door.

"Come, let's get a drink."

THE TAVERN WAS LAID out almost identically to everywhere they'd stayed before, with chambers on the upper levels and a common gathering room on the ground floor.

The friends avoided sitting at the bar—the heart of the chaos—and settled in a ring of chairs around the fire. They were clearly coveted, but between the fae and the vampire, no one dared to approach. They were able to relax in relative peace, sipping drinks and watching those around them.

Considering the size of the valley, it wasn't a varied clientele. Most of the people had clearly descended from men, as Eden had said before, but there were quite a few shifters. Kiera was both surprised and pleased that she was able to recognize them—even without the extra senses of her magical friends. Perhaps it was because they moved so much like Jesse did himself.

Fluid, but assertive. Confident. With surprisingly quick hands.

We should have gotten a second room.

Her cheeks flamed with a sudden blush, although she hadn't said a word out loud. Yet her eyes strayed to the armchairs across the fire, thinking the others might not be opposed themselves.

Even when the vampire and the fae weren't together, they were never far apart. When one reached for something, the other had it waiting. When one leaned forward, the other eased back. It was like they were tied by some invisible string, always moving in tandem with one another.

There was something about it that seemed almost private, though it couldn't help but draw Kiera's eyes. It felt very much like what the vampire had said—to witness such tenderness was a gift.

Even now, they had drawn their chairs together—indifferent to the eyes of the room.

Eden was tracing the rim of his glass, watching some men play dice on the other side of the room, while Evander was reclining with an arm draped loosely across his shoulders. His eyes drifted aimlessly, as he stroked a finger along the shell of the fae's ear, tapping lightly against the point.

Kiera followed the movement jealously, having wanted to do the exact thing many times herself. She was about to make a joke to that effect, when the vampire looked suddenly towards her.

"He is *mine*."

Within a second, the temperature seemed to spike several hundred degrees. Kiera stared in shock, thinking he must be joking or she had somehow misheard, but a single look at the vampire's face told her otherwise. His arm tightened territorially, and those dark eyes burned into hers with exactly as much silent intensity as she'd been watching them with just a moment before.

"No, I wasn't—" she stammered, shaking her head in confusion. "I was just—"

But as fate would have it, the fight would not be hers.

"What was that?" Eden leaned forward, a dangerous smile playing about his face. Evander's arm fell to the chair behind him, as the two locked eyes. "I must have misheard."

It was the second time he'd used that particular phrase, and the fae was still having trouble letting go of the first. The others flushed awkwardly, but the vampire was completely unabashed.

"You are mine," he said plainly. "It is nothing but the truth."

Eden nodded slowly, never breaking his gaze.

"Yours..." he repeated, with a chilling smile. "Like a horse or a pocket-watch. Something with slightly higher value, I'd hope. Something belonging to you."

The vampire watched in silence as he pushed to his feet.

"The next time you feel tempted to say something like that," he continued softly, "to reduce me to property, something owned...I want you to think about a horse or a pocket-watch."

He gave the vampire a parting look.

"Then I want you to strike yourself in the face."

The chair pushed back loudly as Eden stormed across the tavern—flinging open the door and slamming it behind him. The sound was lost in the clamor, but the friends flinched all the same.

Evander was merely lost, staring after him.

"...what must I do now?"

There was something so completely bewildered about him in moments like this, that despite the strange accusation, the others couldn't help but feel the slightest bit protective.

Of a *vampire*. How the world had changed.

Jesse leaned back in his chair, stretching his arms above his head. "You must apologize."

The vampire let out a breath, pushing slowly to his feet. The last few days had been full of such lessons, but each one seemed to end exactly the same. "You people spend a lot of time apologizing, don't you?"

The shifter flashed a grin. "You have no idea."

With a parting nod, the vampire swept quickly across the tavern, vanishing in the same direction as the fae. The others looked after them before Jesse pushed to his feet as well.

"I'll get us some drinks."

Kiera nodded in silence, curling her legs beneath her and staring over the crowd.

Unlike most of the other taverns she'd seen, this one bore at least some claim to being a family establishment. As she sat there, a group of shifters wandered down the stairs. There was a man and a woman, along with a high-spirited little boy. The woman kissed the child on the cheek, murmuring something that he dutifully ignored, before his father swept him upon his shoulders.

There was a chorus of laughter, then they slipped further into the crowd. She stared after them for a long time after, watching without realizing, her hand propped up beneath her chin.

Not long before, the fae had asked where she intended to go when the quest was finally completed and their lives were once again their own. They'd been wandering through a lovely forest, she'd been utterly enchanted, and he'd asked if that's where she might wish to remain.

It was a simple enough question, one that most people could have answered without a second thought. But try as she might, she couldn't come up with a single thing to say in reply.

I cannot go home. My home was destroyed.

These words, at least, were familiar. In the weeks following the attack on Cattaling, she used to chant them to herself each night before falling asleep. It had been a way of keeping grounded, a way of reminding herself what had happened—like she could ever forget. A silly trick, perhaps, but the fire had been too great a thing to hold inside her head. She'd needed a way to make it real.

These days, that void had been filled with other things. So many other things, full days went by without her remembering the smoke. But what happened when those things were gone?

The fae and the vampire would stay together, of this she had no doubt.

Since Eden was physically incapable of holding still, and Evander was physically incapable of leaving him, they would probably wander from one corner of the realm to another.

Always set on another adventure. Always reaching for the other's hand.

And what about me?

They were falling in love, there was no place for her there. And while the little fellowship may have formed an unlikely bond, the immortals had little in common with a mortal girl.

And what about Jesse?

Her eyes drifted in the opposite direction, finding him easily in the crowd.

For all her years of aimless daydreams, for all her endless questions, she could never have counted on something quite like Jesse. He seemed both the end and the beginning, as if the time in the middle had just been waiting—pining in silence for a person she had never met.

They had shared firsts, and shared fires. They had fought and reconciled. They had taken up the greatest burden their world had to offer, and lifted it together with both hands.

He always smiled when he saw her coming. He always made her smile as well.

Would he stay with me when this is over? Is that something I even want?

Although she had no way of knowing it, the shifter had been rather preoccupied with the same questions himself. He'd finished paying for the drinks and was carrying them back, when an old man tumbled out of nowhere—knocking them precariously in his hands.

"I'm sorry!" he croaked, grabbing onto the wolf for balance. "So sorry!" He righted himself a second later, fixing his shirt with a grin. "Careful with that whiskey, my boy. It catches up to you!"

Whiskey. Fantastic.

Jesse laughed and slipped past him, rejoining her beside the fire.

"You need to be more careful," she teased, taking a tankard from his hand. "He was about nine thousand years old. You could have killed him."

He settled in the adjacent chair. "My apologies."

He lifted his own glass and they clinked together—proceeding to drink. Rather, she forced herself to drink, while he watched over the rim of his glass with a secret grin.

"You hate it."

"I do," she admitted, wiping her mouth. The whiskey had burned all the way down her throat, leaving a scorched trail behind it. "I don't know how you can drink that stuff."

He leaned forward with a grin and swapped their glasses—drinking deeply, as she stared down in surprise. Juice. He'd gotten juice in preparation for her inevitable judgement.

She peered down with a smile, swishing it around.

Then all at once, it slipped from her face.

"When Eden was caught in the worst of the fever," she began quietly, "when he thought that he might..." She trailed off for a moment, then lifted her eyes. "He asked me to kill him."

Jesse turned slowly, his face still with shock.

For a few seconds, he was unable to think of anything to say in reply. When he finally managed to speak, the only thing he could do was deny it.

"He was burning with fever. He did not mean it—"

"He did."

She played it back in her mind, fingers drumming manically against the glass. Since the fae had given her a blade and made his request, she'd never really stopped thinking about it. No matter how many days had passed. No matter how well the remedy had worked. Not for a single instant had it fully left her mind. It was something she hadn't realized until that very moment.

She spoke quickly now, like she needed to purge the thoughts from her mind.

"He hand me a knife and told me to do it swiftly. He showed me where. He said Evander would stay with us afterward, see our journey through to the end—"

"He wouldn't," Jesse interrupted, turning to stare across the tavern. "It is the thing I fear most. The narrow scope of the vampire's sentiment. He would stay for Eden, not for us."

She leaned back with a touch of surprise, worried to discover a part of her agreed. "You heard what he said after we found the glass village. He committed himself to our cause—"

"But his feeling for Eden grows with each sunrise. He would be broken if anything were to happen. I believe the world could burn down around him, and he wouldn't notice until it was gone."

Again...she agreed.

They turned their minds to other things, deliberately letting the subject rest. Glasses were lifted and slowly drained. The fire crackled loud and warm beside them.

It was a long while before either of them spoke again.

"Jess...can I ask you something about the binding?"

He glanced over in surprise, having been staring unblinkingly into the fire. "Of course."

She colored with a preemptive blush, fingers twisting nervously inside her sleeves.

"It's not like—" The words caught in her throat and she took a breath to steady herself, flashing him a swift look. "It's not like a marriage, is it? Or a proposal?"

His lips parted in amazement. "Why on earth would you think that?"

Her blush deepened even further, like crushed berries. "I didn't really, it's just...you said that your parents had done it, and every other couple, and it happened so quickly that I never...I never really asked you what it's supposed to mean."

She certainly *felt* what it was supposed to mean. She'd *felt* it every day since it happened. But she wanted to hear him say it, in his own words. Then maybe she could find the words herself.

Sure enough, he didn't disappoint.

"It means you have a piece of me," he said simply, "and you have it forever. Whether we stay in each other's lives, or find ourselves drifting apart. You have changed me in a way that can't be undone. In a way I would never wish to be undone." He opened his mouth to say more, then closed it with a little smile. "It was your birthday. I wanted to give you something in return."

Her pulse steadied, then quickened. That blush spread over her like wildfire, igniting the rest of her skin, and for whatever reason, she found herself looking again at his hands.

Say something. Say something in return.

"...oh."

Her eyes snapped shut as the tiny voice inside her head went sour. *Well done.*

Minutes crawled by as they sat there in silence, though neither was as distracted as they'd been before. Quite the contrary, each one was hyperaware of the other. Each one was playing back every word that had just been spoken, wondering at better things they might have said instead.

After a deceptively long while, he flashed a sudden grin.

"You thought I had proposed?" he asked, shaking with silent laughter. "And as a wolf, no less. You thought I had proposed without speaking. And then, just...not told you?" He bit his lip as that laughter threatened to break free. "Like I was hoping you wouldn't notice we were engaged?"

Every word might have been true, but she refused to admit it.

"You are famously self-centered," she countered stiffly. "I would expect nothing else."

Their eyes met, warming with a shared smile.

A second later, he pulled their chairs closer together, reaching for her hand.

"If we're being honest, I'm actually glad you said something." His fingers traced the length of hers before lacing themselves in between. "Ever since that day, I've regretted the way that it happened. It was so abrupt. I didn't really know how to explain."

His eyes drifted to the window, lingering a moment in the dark.

"It isn't easy to feel the way I feel for you, to say the things I wish to say, when we're always in the company of other people." He shivered suddenly, like he was fighting off a chill. "I believe in what we're doing, but sometimes I wish that...I wish that it was already..."

He lifted slowly to his feet, eyes fixed upon the window. "Kiera, do you...?"

The glass slipped from his hands, shattering into a hundred pieces

"Seven hells!"

Chapter 13

Jesse did not stop to explain before racing from the tavern. He also didn't stop for people.

He'd stood there a second longer, like a bird poised on the verge of flight, then without a hint of warning, he sprinted straight through the crowd—leaving the glass clattering behind him.

Kiera jumped in her skin, staring after him in shock. It took a second for her wits to return, then she took off after him, apologizing desperately to everyone he'd shoved out of the way.

It can't be the dragon. More people would be screaming if it was the dragon.

Her mind spun with a hundred terrifying prospects, as she knocked her way clumsily to the door, each one even worse than the last. So many creatures they'd faced in the span of only a few weeks, so many nightmares to choose from. It might have been a blisserin or a troll. It might have been another company of Carpathians, or maybe his old pack had found him after all.

She slid to a breathless stop behind him, prepared for anything.

But she could never have guessed the next thing that came out of his mouth.

"Emery."

The shifter was standing right in front of her, trembling head to toe. His whole body was screaming, but he could manage nothing more than a whisper, staring in astonishment at the trees.

He turned around a second later, breathless tears sliding down his face.

"I cannot believe it...my brother is alive!"

Kiera stared at Jesse. Then she stared into the shadows behind him. There was nothing there.

His shouts had carried, and soon other people poured curiously out of the tavern, staring at him strangely and talking behind cupped hands. The shifter never saw them. His eyes were only for his brother. The one who had been murdered in the middle of childhood, only a year before.

"Em...it's all right. Nothing will harm you now. It's just me." He took a faltering step closer, reaching out a hand. "Why do you hide in the shadows? Come here, let me see you."

His skin was so pale, it looked cold to the touch.

His voice was so tender, it tore at Kiera's heart.

She stood rigid behind him, flying through the last few days in her mind.

He wasn't touched by the cougar, they'd eaten none of the meat. He hadn't even moved it off the trail—they had left it frothing where it lay. And yet...?

Eden and Evander appeared a second later, drawn by the noise.

"What is it?" the fae asked quickly. "What's happened?"

She turned to him, stricken. "It's his brother," she whispered, clutching at his sleeve. "He thinks—"

"Eden!" Jesse was overjoyed, gesturing him forward. "Come and meet someone. This is my brother, Emery. I cannot understand what happened. I was so sure..."

He trailed into silence, unwilling to say anything more. There was no longer a need. His sweet brother had been returned to him. Wearing the same smile. Wearing the same clothes.

The fae stepped cautiously forward. "Jesse...I cannot see him."

"What? What do you mean, you cannot *see* him?" The shifter was so breathless with elation, he actually laughed. "He is standing right before you! Have you gone blind?"

Kiera cupped a hand over her mouth, tears spilling down her own cheeks as well.

How cruel are the gods? He will not get through this a second time.

Eden stepped even closer, resting a gentle hand upon the wolf's arm.

"I cannot see him," he repeated softly. "Are you looking at him now?"

The second the men touched, everything shattered apart. The illusion vanished and whatever the shifter had been staring at, whatever had made him so desperately happy...disappeared.

He blinked quickly and a chill came over his face. His eyes flew back to the forest, searching.

"Emery...?" He took a step forward, reaching his hand into the air like they might touch. "I don't understand." His voice swelled in volume, then fell to a whisper. "He was right here..."

Eden threw a quick glance over his shoulder, and Evander spoke a few short words to the crowd. A few short words was all you'd ever need from a vampire. Without a pause, they began to disperse—heads bowed in deferential silence, melting into doorways and easing into shops.

The fae circled slowly to face him, half a dozen careful steps.

"Jess, are you—"

"Don't TOUCH me!" the shifter cried, reeling away from him. "Don't say ANYTHING!"

He staggered back with a dry sob, clutching his chest as wild tears flew off his face. The other hand, he raised like a shield between them—trembling so hard, he could hardly keep it up.

"I am NOT mad, Eden!" he shouted, painfully aware that's exactly something a person touched by madness might say. "Don't you DARE touch me! I know what you asked of Kiera. I know what you made her promise to do. You will NOT do the same to me!"

Without another word, he took off running straight back to the tavern—bypassing the main chamber altogether and leaping up the stairs. He didn't stop moving until he was back in their room.

They heard the door slam from outside.

...what in seven hells just happened?

"What is he talking about?" Evander asked quietly. "What did you make her promise to do?"

The fae visibly stiffened, as Kiera braced beside him.

"We will speak on it later," he answered, eyes drifting up to the tavern windows. They were all lit with candles, glowing from within. All except one. "Right now, we have bigger problems..."

THE THREE FRIENDS CLIMBED the stairs together, ghosting down the hallway only to find the door was already unlocked. They pushed it open and saw the shifter sitting on the side of the bed.

They had been relieved that he'd headed for the tavern. It would have been quite another thing to track down a wolf in the woods—perhaps even impossible, given his state of mind.

But looking at him now, that relief vanished on the spot.

The coals were still smoldering in the hearth from the remains of a fire, heating the room almost unbearably, but despite how close he sat, Jesse was trembling. His skin was shock pale, damp with a faint sheen, as though a fever had lifted, and his roving eyes had fixed upon a single spot.

How can we help him? How does one come back from such a thing?

Kiera pulled in a breath, then sat down beside him—lifting a gentle hand and placing it on his back. He was cold, but hot at the same time. She rubbed slow circles, wondering how she would react to the sudden appearance of Talbot or Marcel, or anyone else from her village.

If she was being honest, she'd probably faint on the spot.

"When my brother died, in those days afterwards...I saw him." His voice was quiet, yet still it carried. The others exchanged a quick glance, surprised he could even speak.

Kiera leaned closer and mimicked his posture, both arms resting on her knees. "Like a ghost?" she asked softly. "Or a dream?"

He shook his head.

"The same as I'm seeing you now" His hands were still shaking, clenched into fists. "There would be flashes of him in a window, glimpses of his face in a crowd. Sometimes when I'd turn, he would still be there. Just for a moment. But he would *be* there...until the moment he was not."

Like the flicker of a dream, she remembered what he'd told her in the days just after they'd met, about how he understood how it felt to have a story that other people wouldn't believe. She'd been curious at the time, but her head was still spinning with the dragon.

She'd always framed their meeting like that, thinking what a strange point it had been in her own life. Not until that very moment did she realize what a point it had been in his.

Eden nodded slowly, settling on the ground by his knees.

Perhaps it was merely to listen. Perhaps it was a casual way to ensure his friend didn't shift after all and vanish into the woods without a trace.

"Tell me more."

Jesse flashed him a quick look and wiped brusquely at his cheeks, coming back to himself enough to look self-conscious for the first time. "What's the point? You already think I'm crazy."

"I *do not* think you're crazy," the fae replied immediately, placing careful emphasis on each of the words. "I *do not* think it. Many years I've wandered this place, and many people I have lost. Each one is different, leaving its own mark. Who am I to say what you saw?" He hesitated a brief moment then added, "I can only tell you...I did not see him myself."

The shifter drew in a deep breath, hands clenched on his knees.

"This time was different," he said quietly. "It was not merely a glimpse of him. He didn't appear, then vanish. This time he stayed." His voice seemed to ache with the word, picking up speed. "The entire time I ran through the tavern, I could see him through the glass. His face wasn't fixed, it brightened when he saw me. He was excited, I think. He was starting to raise his hand…" He trailed into silence, looking down at his own.

Kiera slipped hers inside. "Tell me what you need," she whispered. "Tell me what I can do."

He sat there a second longer, then bowed his head to his chest. *"Stay."*

AFTER WHAT FELT LIKE an eternity, Kiera left Jesse in the bedroom, staring vacantly at the wall.

He had wanted her in the beginning, but he didn't want her by the end. He didn't seem to want anything. Not the fire, not to sleep. Only a little boy, who wasn't there anymore.

She'd kissed him on the cheek before heading down the stairs.

Her arms ached from holding them at such an angle, and there was a pulsing throb in her leg. She reached down to rub it, hands slipping into her pocket, only to realize it wasn't an ache, but a burn. The stone that had been resting upon it was hot to the touch. *Frightfully* hot.

She pulled it out with a frown, turning it slowly over.

Was I pressing on it somehow? Or was I too near the embers of the fire?

The sound of quiet voices roused her, and she slipped it back into her cloak.

Eden and Evander was standing in the middle of the tavern floor, a place that had been graciously deserted after the vampire's pointed words. They had not yet noticed her. From the sound of things, they were having a similar conversation to the one she'd had with herself.

"And he didn't touch the cougar?" Eden asked for the third time. "Not even a scratch?"

Evander gave the same reply. "I was not looking—"

"He wouldn't have touched it," the fae muttered, answering his own question. "And he didn't find anything, when you sent him into the woods? Nothing that might have—"

"He would have told us and that was days ago," the vampire interrupted softly, "it would have taken him by now." He reached a hand between them, resting on the fae's arm. "Eden, there was *no* blood on him when he returned. I would have known. This must have been something else."

Kiera stepped loudly into the room, and two heads snapped up.

"How is he?" Eden asked immediately.

A flash of Jesse's face drifted through her mind.

"Not well. Have you gotten any..." She saw the fresh mud on his boots and looked up in surprise. "You checked for him? You checked the forest?"

Eden flushed, raking back his hair. "I could not in good conscience tell him I *didn't* check. You know what they say of death, it is always hardest on those left behind."

She nodded faintly and turned to the vampire, expecting him to impart some wisdom. He was an expert on such things, after all. But that wisdom fell remarkably short.

"Death is cold," he said flatly. "There is little else to the matter."

Eden's eyes flickered guiltily towards him, but the vampire stared right ahead.

That must have been a fun conversation you two had.

"I don't know what to do for him," she said bluntly. "I don't know what can be done."

Ironically enough, it seemed a much harder fix than any of the fantastical problems that had plagued them before. There had been a woman in her village who'd kept seeing flashings of her dead daughter. After a few months of weeping, she'd thrown herself down the well.

"There is nothing that can be done," Eden admitted, casting a look up the stairs. "At least no comfort that I've ever felt. We can be there for him, we can hold his hand." He let out a tired sigh, shaking his head. "Perhaps if we found out what triggered the memory *this* night, it might be of some use to him..."

The door pushed open, but none of them noticed—they were too distracted by their own conversation to hear the frantic hush of voices coming from the stairs. It wasn't until a person called loudly out across the tavern, they realized they were no longer alone.

"*Kaya.*"

The fae looked up surprise. It was not spoken in the common tongue, but his own. Loosely translated, it meant teacher. But over the years, it had come to mean so much more.

Mentor, counselor, guardian.

It was one of the first words every child of the realm was taught to say.

The second he turned, a group of people rushed towards them, boots scuffing against the floor. There were maybe half a dozen—shifters, by the look of them. All were wearing the same stricken expression, all were looking at the fae as though he was a miracle sent down to earth.

"Please—you must help us!"

There was no slowing of speed as one group collided with the other. One of the men cast off from the rest and threw himself forward, grabbing Eden by the cloak. He clung on the way a child held to its mother, utterly immune to the murderous-looking vampire standing by his side.

"You must help us," he gasped again, tears and sweat pouring down his cheeks. "It is my son! He is missing! All day we have been searching, and I...*I cannot find my son!*"

The man was quickly replaced by a woman, just as distraught. She looked older than the fae by several decades, but immortality had a way of erasing such things. She grasped onto his sleeves.

"*Please,*" she whispered, while her husband shouted, "you are our last hope."

The fae tensed, in a way only his friends would ever notice.

It was not the first time he'd been given such a request, but it was most certainly the first time the others had ever seen it. There was a reckless havoc, almost a selfishness to the way they threw themselves upon him—like he was a celestial parachute, and not a living, breathing man.

Not until later would Kiera realize, she had approached him much the same way.

No wonder they wish to lock themselves away in cities.

There is nothing more exhausting than to carry another's hope.

He took a step back, lifting a subtle hand between them.

"Peace, friends...tell me what happened."

They told a story old as time, the same as so many countless others. Their child had gone for a walk in the forest, as he so often did. Just a quick walk before breakfast, then they would get on with the day. They were going to the lakefront to visit family, and—that part didn't matter. He went for a walk in the forest, and he never returned. All day they had been searching. The boy was gone.

"Now you see, you have to help us!" The father stood up from where Eden had made them sit beside the fire, reaching back down and half-pulling the fae to his feet. "There isn't a moment to be wasted, the sun has already set—"

Evander's cool hand appeared on his wrist.

"Let go of his cloak," he said softly.

The man blinked in surprise, looking down at his own hands. He hadn't realized that he'd grabbed the fae. He released him in a daze. Again, his wife stepped forward.

"There were many travelling along the road with our same story," she muttered urgently, as though she was speaking just to Eden. "*Many* others, within the span of only a few days."

Despite the devastating tale, that part made the most impact.

In most cases, this meant some kind of animal. A raging, unlikely animal. Possibly magical, possibly a few. In other cases, this meant some kind of creature—a subtle distinction that depended on who you asked. Things like banshees or kelpies, ogres or trolls. Things like the handsome man standing at the fae's side. But these were not *most* days, so these were not *most* cases.

The fae could rule nothing out.

"How many more?"

"Over twenty, and those were only the ones with whom we spoke. There could be dozens of others." She wrung her fingers together, so hard as to break the skin. "Will you help us?"

The fae opened his mouth with the natural reply, but the words fell silent on his lips. His eyes flicked back up the stairs, before coming to rest upon Kiera.

"I am sorry for your loss and for your panic," he murmured, fingers curving around the woman's hands. "I have no children, I cannot begin to imagine your pain. And I *will* help you," he added deliberately, "you have my word. But I cannot..." He caught himself, eyes flashing again up the stairs. "A friend of mine is unwell. I cannot—"

"This is a boy of *fifteen*!" the father shouted. "Forget your bloody friend!"

Eden looked at him with unending patience, a profound sympathy tightening his eyes. "My friend is not many years older than that. And there is a chance that something..." He trailed off, letting out a quiet breath. "I swear if you have not found him by tomorrow, I will—"

"Are you joking, Eden?"

Everyone turned at the same time as another man appeared at the base of the stairs. He had been standing there a while, listening in silence. No one had noticed him until now.

Jesse.

He stepped forward, staring at the fae.

"Their son goes missing, the same day I see my dead brother?"

Their eyes locked for a brief moment.
"We leave at dawn."

Chapter 14

The friends did indeed find many others as they travelled further into the mountains. All of them touched with the same tragedy, all of them relieved beyond measure to see a fae already on the trail. They would throw that tragedy on his shoulders, then depart with a feeling of profound relief, as if their own emotional contribution had come to an end. Over and over, all of them did it.

They would have solace, he would have none.

"We should not be doing this," Evander said softly as they stepped through the trees. "We are looking for a dragon. Not this...this is mortal kind of trouble."

There was no longer a path, but they were taking the simplest route—easing gently upwards, just as the missing shifters might have done. In the beginning, they had been looking for tracks, something made by wolves, not men. But their perspective had changed the longer they searched.

Eden threw him a quick look, walking by his side. "I cannot imagine they are not connected," he murmured in reply. "And we are here, and they are in trouble." He said it so simply, catching the vampire's eye. "This is what my people do."

Evander stared a moment, then took his hand. "Then we shall do it together."

Kiera glanced over her shoulder, back towards the little town.

It was harder to see now, lost in the wide sweep of the valley. That tangle of rivers seemed almost to swallow it, glinting like a spiderweb in the sun.

She wondered for the hundredth time, if they should tell someone. If they should not be keeping word of the dragon to themselves. But the same reasons they'd had before, held true that day. People would not mobilize, they would scatter. Some would be picked off immediately, others would fall prey to lesser evils that would not have reached them before. Those who remained in the villages would live in a state of perpetual fear. Clutching their children, staring up at the sky.

Don't worry, I've already told a fae.

"What's the matter, Evander?" Jesse called over his shoulder, hacking away at the dense ferns in his path. "Afraid we'll find some of your kinsmen?"

The shifter had been a bit sharper than usual, and the others were granting him a lot of leeway. The vampire had never heard that particular word. They were explaining as best they could.

"Killing a bunch of vampires..." he continued under his breath, slicing through the swaying branches with his blade. "That would be a real shame."

Evander's face stilled in anger, but Eden was quick to squeeze his hand.

"Let's take a break."

They'd been hiking for the better part of the morning, having left the village at sunrise, just as Jesse said. The day was hot and they'd been moving with a great deal of caution, heading not westward, but into the same forest they'd been before—where they'd seen the infected cougar. It wasn't the greatest of leads, but under the circumstances, it was the best one they had.

Maybe the fae is right. Maybe it's all connected.

"We should probably sweep the perimeter as well," Eden continued, his bright eyes roving through the trees. "If we are looking for trouble, then it's best we find it first."

Jesse nodded briskly, pushing back to his feet. "I'll do it—"

The fae caught his arm.

"Perhaps one of us," he suggested lightly, cocking his head towards Evander. He flashed an apologetic smile, rigid beneath the surface. "Immortal ears."

It was an excuse, and a rather transparent one. Everyone knew a shifter could hear nearly as well as a fae. Eden was simply worried. He didn't want his friend to run off again, slipping into a trance and following the ghost of murdered siblings into the trees.

Kiera stared between them, remembering what he'd said at the tavern. *A friend of mine is unwell. And there is a chance that something...* She would give anything to know what he hadn't said.

She expected Jesse to be angry, but he wasn't. He merely settled down to build a fire.

"You two can take turns. You should be good at that."

The vampire was livid, but the fae merely chuckled under his breath. He stepped again between them, pressing a kiss to Evander's head. "How about I start?"

He was gone a second later, spiriting away into the trees.

The others settled down in the leaves, as a crackling fire sprang to life between them. It was a good thing Evander had decided not to sell the flint. They had use for it after all.

"I'll grab us a bucket of water," Kiera murmured, pushing to her feet. "We passed a stream not so long ago, I can still hear—"

"Now that Eden is gone," Evander interrupted sharply, "is there anything else you'd like to say about vampires or the idea of taking turns?"

On second thought, I think I'll stay.

Jesse stared back in silence, not a shred of emotion on his face.

"He was upset, Evander." Kiera settled back down in between them, just as the fae had done before. "He meant you no offence."

That being said, it didn't look as though Jesse particularly cared. Quite the opposite. And the vampire was not taking to the concept of 'leeway' as well as the others had thought.

After a few seconds, the shifter cocked his head with a dry smile. "You do not like my jokes?"

"I do not like your jokes."

A frosty silence fell between them, one Kiera felt quite certain Eden would have been able to break, if he hadn't chosen that precise moment to vanish into the ether and leave her sitting between two such volatile men. Instead of appealing again to the vampire, she squeezed the shifter's knee.

His shoulders fell with a sigh. He was angry, not suicidal.

"Then I will keep them to myself," he conceded stiffly. "Kiera's right, I didn't mean you any offence. For whatever reason, Eden likes you—"

"He likes me a great deal more than you," the vampire interrupted with a smirk.

"He likes taking your pants off," Jesse answered sharply. "There's a difference. Chalk it up to an over-developed sense of masochism."

A look of uncertainty flashed across Evander's face, and Kiera realized it was possible to wound him after all. At least, about this particular thing. She had thought earlier that at the core of the vampire was pure confidence. But there was nothing confident about him now. He looked as new as a sunburst, as fragile as butterfly wings—just as easy to frighten away.

She was not the only one to see it happen.

"I'm sorry," Jesse murmured, bowing his head. "I did not mean it."

Evander nodded curtly, and they stared in silence at the fire.

Yes...I think you did.

IT WAS ONLY A FEW MINUTES later when Eden returned, holding a trio of freshly-picked apples in his hand. He tossed them quickly around the fire, settling down himself.

"I found nothing but these, though the woods are unusually quiet. Perhaps we might want to consider—" He cut short at the look on Evander's face. "What's the matter? What happened?"

"Nothing."

"Nothing."

The vampire and the shifter spoke at the same time. When Eden turned incredulously to Kiera, she rolled her eyes. "I guess nothing's wrong."

The friends ate quickly, then put out the fire and got back on the trail. There had been no further confrontations, but Jesse made himself deliberately scarce, keeping far to the front.

For almost a mile, Eden stared at the back of his head.

Then he turned again to the vampire.

"What's wrong?" he asked quietly. "Will you please tell me?"

If he'd been talking to anyone else, there was a good chance he wouldn't have gotten an answer. But the vampire didn't know the games, and he wouldn't have played them.

He spoke softly, keeping his eyes on the ground.

"...do you have an over-developed sense of masochism?"

The fae let out a burst of laughter, caught by surprise. "I suppose I do," he answered. "Is there a better way to live?"

In the silence that followed, the smile faded from his face. "Why are you asking?"

More silence. Longer, this time.

"Is that why you're with me?" Evander asked quietly. "Is it the reason we're together?"

Eden stopped moving, right in the center of the trail. He waited there until the vampire stopped as well, then crossed the distance between them and took him by the hands.

"No, that is not why I'm with you." He spoke quietly, each gentle word in stark contrast to the intensity of his gaze. "I am with you for exactly the opposite reason."

Evander avoided his eyes, answering with a hint of reluctance. "And what is that?"

Eden reached out with a smile, lifting the vampire's chin. "There is a light inside you, Evander. It might not be well-tended, but it's there."

His eyes twinkled in the rising sun. "It is that light that draws me closer."

THE FRIENDS HIKED UNTIL dusk.

The slope got steadily higher, and the woods were just as empty as the fae had said. Even the birds were silent. It was a little unnerving, like the cresting of a wave about to break.

"I was hoping to find something before nightfall," Eden murmured after a long stretch of silence, lifting his eyes towards the sky. "But the sun is already sinking. It will be dark before long."

Kiera shivered in spite of herself.

He was hoping to find *something*. It might not have been said directly, but he no longer believed they would find any of the shifters alive. She was starting to agree.

"I could always start calling for them," Evander said casually, hiking along beside them. "If the culprit truly is one of us barbaric vampires, they might just follow the sound of my voice."

Eden cast him a tired look, but said nothing.

The fae's earlier words had soothed away the worry, brightening the vampire in a way he didn't expect. But that had been hours ago, and he'd had more than enough time to sink back into a miserable introspective. The longer they were silent, the worse it seemed to become.

"Of course, there's a chance they won't understand," he continued, beheading dandelions with a flick of his hand. "Most of us don't speak the common tongue, or any other language. We communicate solely through blood rituals and strategic glares."

The fae let out a slow breath, searching for patience.

"Oh yes?" he quipped. "How about a demonstration? Let's see if you can walk in stoic silence for the rest of the way."

On second thought, the fae weren't known for their patience.

Evander shot him such a look, and the others were convinced there was something to the glaring after all. Not one to be dissuaded, he stepped up his game.

"If that's what you wish," he replied stiffly. "If it helps, I can always return to the tavern and wait for you there. Gods forbid you're seen in the company of such a creature—"

"Enough!" Eden whirled around in exasperation, stopping the group in its tracks. "Why do you put that on me? When you know I do not think it. When you know the only person voicing that opinion is yourself. A ceaseless worry that troubles only one man, is not a shared problem, Evander. Whatever weight there is to bear, you bear it yourself. Such talk is beneath us and I will not hear it." He stormed ahead without a backward glance, unaware of the others staring behind him.

"A ceaseless worry that troubles only one man, is not a shared problem," Jesse repeated with a crooked grin. "Why do you always speak as though you've swallowed a book of proverbs?"

The fae threw him a cold look, never slowing his pace.

"Where do you think proverbs come from? There is a reason my people were granted an eternity and tasked with defending this world. Timeless words of wisdom come with the—"

There was a rush of leaves, followed by a panicked shout.

Then the fae was dangling in the air.

"Eden!"

Evander lunged forward, actually catching the tip of the fae's fingers—but he released him just as fast, taking a moment to assess the situation before stepping back with a little smile.

"Well, look at you..."

It was a net, Kiera realized, lowering her hands slowly from her mouth. A massive, twisting net that had been hidden in the leaves. It was the kind of thing that the more skilled hunters had used around her village when they could afford to buy the rope. The kind of thing that

Eden would have seen in a heartbeat, if he hadn't been so busy extolling the enduring wisdom of the fae.

She gave him a little push, watching as he swung back and forth. *"Get me down from here!"*

But the fae's friends were no longer listening. In fact, it was safe to say they were no longer his friends. He was their prisoner now, hanging upside-down in an inexorable tangle, only little pieces of him still visible, with the tips of his long hair dusting the leaves.

Jesse cast a look towards the heavens, lips curling in a little grin. "Did you do that just for me?"

Eden cried out in frustration, cursing in his native tongue. "Evan, come here!" he demanded, reaching helplessly for the vampire's hands. For a second, it looked like he might have gotten close enough. Then the breeze swung him the other way. "This is intolerable!" He cursed again, fighting against the rope. "If I had not been distracted—"

"It is a poor craftsman who blames his tools," Kiera said sagely.

Eden rotated slowly towards her, white with rage. *"Get. Me. Down."*

Jesse patted him on the leg. "In time," he promised. "They say patience is bitter, but its fruits are sweet."

There was another vengeful cry.

"Do not PROVERB at me!"

But there was no point. The fae's weapons had fallen to the ground, and a force larger than himself was keeping him still. The others proceeded to 'proverb' at him to their hearts' delight.

The only one who didn't partake was the vampire.

Evander was watching in silence, arms folded across his chest and a twinkle of amusement in his eyes.

When the fae swung slowly towards him, he tilted his head with a sweet smile. "Would you like something to drink?"

The pair of them locked eyes.

"Get me down...*now.*"

The vampire didn't move. "I'm getting ideas for later."

"Malecos!"

The fae struggled violently against the mess of knots, levelling every bit of that immortal strength, only to find himself in exactly the same position as when he started. He gave up only a moment later, more twisted than when he'd started and panting for breath.

"I guarantee you'll be enjoying them by yourself, if you do not *free me from these ropes*!"

Kiera folded her arms, surveying him appraisingly. "I remember a time when you wanted to string me up like that," she remarked. "How did you phrase it? Ah yes, you wanted to use me as bait to 'catch the larger predators.'"

Evander smiled fondly. "We have more and more in common."

"ENOUGH!"

Perhaps it was an act of mercy, or perhaps fear of the fae's inevitable retribution, but Jesse took out his knife and slashed the rope in a few strategic places. There was a shuddering from the branches above, then the entire thing collapsed, spilling the fae to the ground with it.

He landed on his knees, taking a second to recover himself, before shaking off the lingering strands and pushing to his feet. His cheeks were flushed, while the rest of him was literally trembling with fury. His eyes lifted slowly to his friends, resting a moment upon each one.

"I'm going to make you a promise. By sundown tomorrow—"

There was a rush of air, followed by a streak of shadow.

Then the fae vanished again.

"EDEN!"

This time, the rest of them flew into action.

Kiera raced after the others, not seeing what they were seeing, only hearing the signs of a violent struggle. Yips and snarls. Sharp impacts and a distant cry of pain. By the time she pushed through the ferns and into the open air, she could not believe what she was seeing.

Eden was pinned to the ground by a vampire...who was *not* Evander.

"Caros!" he cried, pushing wildly against it. His weapons were still lying on the forest floor, and he was holding it back with nothing but the strength of his bare hands. "Someone—"

Evander was there a second later, flying into the clearing at such speed that his feet scarcely touched the ground. The only reason he hadn't gotten there sooner, was because the vampire had taken the precaution of striking him first. His head was still spinning. But his eyes were clear.

Seven hells!

He tackled the vampire with such force, the others felt the impact in their shoes, hurling it away from Eden and to the other side of the clearing. It wasn't until the creature landed that Kiera got a look at it for the first time. Her, she realized in shock. The vampire was a woman.

She looked very much like Evander, while also looking entirely different.

The two of them were alike in beauty and coloring, but she was slight of stature, with a mane of wild hair that had been tied back with a string. Both feet were bare and bloody—either from her struggle with the fae, or simply from walking through the woods. Her eyes were different as well.

There was something deeply unsettling about her eyes.

She landed on her feet and whipped right back around, preparing to launch herself once more at the fae. But the fight was already finished. She would never get the chance.

With a single hand, Evander picked her up by the back of the neck and cratered her into the earth, shaking the surrounding trees. Her eyelids fluttered as he placed a knee upon her chest, baring his fangs with an expression that was sure to give his friends nightmares for years to come.

In spite of everything, she was still reaching, *always* reaching, for Eden. Those dark eyes of hers were dilated almost completely black, but there was a manic light at the core.

Evander had a solution for that as well.

There was a blistering roar, followed by a distressing *rip*, as he wrapped his fingers around those offending arms—the ones that had struck against his lover—and gave them a mighty tug.

They severed at the shoulders, like a doll tearing apart at the seams.

She died quickly after that. Screaming until the very end.

And then...*nothing.*

A deafening silence fell over the clearing, pulsing like a heartbeat in each of their ears. It froze each one like some kind of spell. Jesse was still gripping his blade, but his fingers had gone loose around the handle. Kiera was just a step behind him, arms hanging limp by her sides.

No matter how long she stood there, no matter how much time had passed, she couldn't seem to reconcile the image. Like her eyes and her brain were unable to force it together.

She is dead. She is dead...in so many pieces.

Eden was still lying on the ground, half-cratered into it. His clothes were torn and his face was shock-white. But his eyes were clear as well—fixed upon a single thing.

"Evander?"

The vampire whipped around with a snarl, curved over the body like an animal defending its kill. That same frenzy still gripped him, but he went instantly quiet when his eyes fell upon the fae.

He took an instinctive step towards him, but stopped himself almost as fast.

The fangs deliberately retracted. The coiled fingers were smoothed on his legs. His lips fluttered in silence, almost as though he was counting. Then he drew in a steadying breath.

"Are you all right?"

No, the fae was most certainly not alright. But it was clear from a look, the vampire was not all right himself. Eden hitched onto his elbows, unable to fully catch his breath.

"I'm fine."

Evander was at his side a moment later, fixing his clothes and checking for damage, lifting him higher and cupping a supportive hand behind his head. The two leaned closer, angling their faces like they were going to kiss. But Eden pulled back at the last moment.

"There's blood...on your mouth."

With those words, the stillness that gripped the clearing shattered. The others drew shakily closer, clinging to each other's hands, as Evander wiped his face with the back of his sleeve.

"None of it is mine," he muttered. "It was all hers."

The fae nodded, eyes on the ground.

"Was she the one who did this?" Kiera asked breathlessly, taking great pains *not* to look at the pieces of the vampire scattered across the ground. "Was she the one who placed the net?"

The men glanced up at the same time, having not yet strung it together. After all their teasing, after all their searching, could it have been a vampire they were looking for after all?

"A vampire does not set traps," Evander murmured with a frown, "but they can scavenge from them." His eyes flashed back through the forest, finding the dented leaves where the creature had sat. "She has been here a while, feeding on whatever animals strayed into the net."

He opened his mouth to say more, then went abruptly still.

Which means...

"She was touched with the same madness," Kiera whispered in horror, remembering the crazed look in the vampire's eyes. "It's why she couldn't control herself. It's why—"

Evander rounded immediately upon the fae.

"Did she bite you?" he asked urgently. "Or scratch you with her nails? Even a little?"

Eden shook his head, still shaken to the core. "No, I...I don't think so."

It was not a good enough answer. With a lot less delicacy than he'd used before, the vampire checked for himself—running hands over every inch of him, combing through his hair. Not until his hands came up clean, did he manage to take a breath.

"There is nothing," he exhaled in relief. "Not a drop of blood."

Eden extracted himself painfully, lifting to his feet.

"But *something* set the trap. *Something* has been here." His eyes drifted further up the mountain. "We have to be getting close."

IT WASN'T UNTIL LONG after nightfall, the friends finally decided to make camp. None of them had wanted to stay in the open, but none of them wanted to be in remote proximity to the net.

Whatever or whoever was pulling the strings, had a very long reach.

They needed to find them. But they would do it in the day.

"This is a better place than most," Eden said wearily, pausing beside an outcropping of rocks and glancing into the shallow cave. "Easily guarded, though I don't imagine we'll be here long."

Kiera paused behind him, peering into the dark. "Could someone—"

"We'll check for bears."

The answer came back from three different directions. Even the vampire had chimed in, though his eyes remained fixed on the forest behind them, searching through the shadowy trees.

"I will keep watch."

This was not a question. The others didn't challenge it.

They didn't have the time or energy to collect wood for a fire, or perhaps each of them was too secretly rattled to venture from the cave. However she tried to distract herself, Kiera couldn't stop remembering the scene from the forest. The way the two vampires collided together, shaking the ground beneath them. The sound of ripping flesh when Evander tore her to pieces.

The look on his face when Eden called his name.

In a way, it had been the most frightening moment of all. She'd been half-convinced Evander was going to attack him. The vampire had been half-convinced himself.

"Are you all right?" he asked for the hundredth time. "Truly?"

Since leaving the bloody mess behind them, he couldn't stop asking the question—nor could he seem to remove himself from Eden's side. The slightest breath was enough to draw his attention, the faintest wince brought his eyes. It would have been almost comical, if the situation wasn't so serious. As it stood, the fae was making a concerted effort to keep from wringing his neck.

"I'm fine, Evander."

"But your shoulder—"

"My shoulder is fine."

The vampire nodded and swept silently from the cave—running a quick check of the perimeter before settling in the mouth of the cave to guard the others so they could sleep.

Jesse waited until he was gone before glancing back at the fae. "...how's your shoulder?"

Eden's eyes flashed up sharply before warming with a smile. "It's probably broken. Hurts like hell." He stretched it in front of him, settling on the floor of the cave. "How's your face?"

The second the danger had passed, Eden had walked calmly up to both the shifter and the vampire, and struck them both across the face. Retribution, for leaving him in the net.

Kiera had not been struck. He'd shoved her into a tree.

"Oh, you know." Jesse settled down beside him. "Really bad."

The two waited expectantly until Kiera settled beside them. She hadn't said much since the incident with the vampire. Both were feeling rather protective, given the look on her face.

"You had never seen one before?" Eden asked softly. "Aside from Evander?"

Her eyes tightened around the edges, then she shook her head.

There was much to say about it. Probably too much. But she didn't have the stomach for it now. She was still trying to reconcile that she lived in a world where people *could* be torn to pieces.

And Evander...he didn't even blink an eye.

"I'm sorry for asking you to do this," Jesse said unexpectedly, remembering his sharp words at the tavern for the fae. "I didn't think it would..." He trailed off, bowing his head. "I'm sorry."

Eden regarded him with a touch of surprise. "You asked for nothing. It was the families of the victims who made the request." His eyes danced with the hint of a smile. "And I don't believe for a second that you're sorry."

The shifter chuckled, rubbing absentmindedly at his face. "Not so much. But I am grateful you would help the others search," he added suddenly. "If someone like you had been closer after Emery...I might have sought you out myself."

If the wolf's day had been difficult before, it became promptly unbearable at the mention of his brother. Without another word, he flashed the others a tight smile and lay down in the corner to go to sleep. Eden joined him not long after, feeling that shoulder a lot more than he was letting on.

By the time Evander returned a few minutes later, Kiera was the only one left awake.

"Did you find anything?" she asked, the moment he stepped inside.

He glanced up in surprise, then shook his head. "Not a single track."

She nodded, feeling strangely unsurprised.

Whatever they were dealing with, wasn't the kind of thing to leave tracks. It was the kind of thing that crazed vampires and lay traps. The kind that raised haunting memories from years past.

It would not leave footprints.

"So I guess we'll find it in the morning."

She said it with as much cheer as she could muster, but there was a chance that didn't quite work. Evander glanced over immediately, making a quick study of her face. He hesitated a moment, inwardly debating, then to her intense surprise, he slipped his arms around her in a fleeting embrace.

"We'll find it in the morning."

THE FRIENDS WENT TO sleep shortly after, that was their first mistake.

Their second was thinking they would be allowed to wake.

They didn't notice when the breeze picked up, filling the cave with a strange and dizzying scent. They didn't notice when their attention started to waver, when things began to muddle and the conversation no longer made sense. They didn't notice when they dropped onto the stone, one after another. And they didn't notice the old man from the tavern standing outside.

"Wake up, darling, it's time to go..."

The shifter rose from the heart of a deep slumber, a blank expression smoothing the edges of his face. His eyes glassed over and his limbs went docile—lifting him like a puppet on a string. In a daze, he stepped over the sleeping vampire and out of the cavern, into a pair of waiting arms.

His friends never saw the look of surprise, or heard the muted struggle. The quickening of breathing, and the quiet tearing of clothes. By the time they opened their eyes the next morning, the world and everything in it was exactly as it should be. There was just one notable exception.

Jesse was gone.

THE END

Disavow Blurb

YOU NEVER KNOW WHAT you have, until it's gone...

When the friends wake up and Jesse is missing, they tear the realm apart trying to find him. But their enemy travels on light footsteps and he may be closer than they think.

It is a race against the clock, as the world begins to slowly unravel. A twisting shadow is creeping over the kingdoms, consuming everything that stands before it, and not everyone finds themselves on the same side. While dragon circles ever above them, Kiera finds herself facing a much smaller problem and a much different kind of question.

They had believed Marrow had done nothing to help them, but perhaps they had been mistaken. Perhaps he had been helping them all along. Perhaps he'd even given them the solution.

Something powerful enough to help them. Something small enough to fit inside a pocket.

Beginning's End Series

Beginnings
Curiosity
Scrutiny
Foresight
Disavow
Trickery
Wisdom
Decree
Influence
Prevail
Dignified
Honored

The Queen's Alpha Series

Eternal

Everlasting

Unceasing

Evermore

Forever

Boundless

Prophecy

Protected

Foretelling

Revelation

Betrayal

Resolved

The Omega Queen Series

Discipline
Bravery
Courage
Conquer
Strength
Validation
Approval
Blessing
Balance
Grievance
Enchanted
Gratified

Find W.J. May

Website:

http://www.wjmaybooks.com

Facebook:

https://www.facebook.com/pages/Author-WJ-May-FAN-PAGE/141170442608149

Newsletter:

SIGN UP FOR W.J. May's Newsletter to find out about new releases, updates, cover reveals and even freebies!

https://www.wjmaybooks.com/subscribe

More books by W.J. May

Hidden Secrets Saga:
Download Seventh Mark part 1 For FREE
BOOK TRAILER:

http://www.youtube.com/watch?v=Y-_vVYC1gvo

Like most teenagers, Rouge is trying to figure out who she is and what she wants to be. With little knowledge about her past, she has questions but has never tried to find the answers. Everything changes when she befriends a strangely intoxicating family. Siblings Grace and Michael, appear to have secrets which seem connected to Rouge. Her hunch is confirmed when a horrible incident occurs at an outdoor party. Rouge may be the only one who can find the answer.

An ancient journal, a Sioghra necklace and a special mark force life-altering decisions for a girl who grew up unprepared to fight for her life or others.

All secrets have a cost and Rouge's determination to find the truth can only lead to trouble...or something even more sinister.

RADIUM HALOS - THE SENSELESS SERIES
Book 1 is FREE

Everyone needs to be a hero at one point in their life.

The small town of Elliot Lake will never be the same again.

Caught in a sudden thunderstorm, Zoe, a high school senior from Elliot Lake, and five of her friends take shelter in an abandoned uranium mine. Over the next few days, Zoe's hearing sharpens drastically, beyond what any normal human being can detect. She tells her friends, only to learn that four others have an increased sense as well. Only Kieran, the new boy from Scotland, isn't affected.

Fashioning themselves into superheroes, the group tries to stop the strange occurrences happening in their small town. Muggings, break-ins, disappearances, and murder begin to hit too close to home. It leads the team to think someone knows about their secret - someone who wants them all dead.

An incredulous group of heroes. A traitor in the midst. Some dreams are written in blood.

Courage Runs Red
The Blood Red Series
Book 1 is FREE

WHAT IF COURAGE WAS your only option?

When Kallie lands a college interview with the city's new hot-shot police officer, she has no idea everything in her life is about to change. The detective is young, handsome and seems to have an unnatural ability to stop the increasing local crime rate. Detective Liam's particular interest in Kallie sends her heart and head stumbling over each other.

When a raging blood feud between vampires spills into her home, Kallie gets caught in the middle. Torn between love and family loyalty she must find the courage to fight what she fears the most and possibly risk everything, even if it means dying for those she loves.

Daughter of Darkness - Victoria
Only Death Could Stop Her Now
The Daughters of Darkness is a series of female heroines who may or may not know each other, but all have the same father, Vlad Montour. Victoria is a Hunter Vampire

Don't miss out!

Visit the website below and you can sign up to receive emails whenever W.J. May publishes a new book. There's no charge and no obligation.

https://books2read.com/r/B-A-SSF-BBVXB

Did you love *Foresight*? Then you should read *Twist and Turns*[1] by W.J. May!

Forgetting is easy. Remembering is hard.

A Fae determined to recover her memory and learn her place in the realm discovers that there are no simple answers.

With the help of a soldier with secrets of his own, she charts a course between two worlds, a dark forest where no Fae dare set foot, and the capital of the realm, which might end up being more deadly.

Can she uncover her identity before the rest of the realm's secrets pull her into something she can't talk or fight her way out of...?

Fae Wilds Series

Twist & TurnsCurse of the FaeForce the TruthCrown & GloryEnemy & RivalsLight in the Dark

---

1. https://books2read.com/u/bx1kgJ

2. https://books2read.com/u/bx1kgJ

Also by W.J. May

Beginning's End Series
Beginnings
Curiosity
Scrutiny
Foresight
Disavow

Blood Red Series
Courage Runs Red
The Night Watch
Marked by Courage
Forever Night
The Other Side of Fear
Blood Red Box Set Books #1-5

Daughters of Darkness: Victoria's Journey
Victoria
Huntress
Coveted (A Vampire & Paranormal Romance)
Twisted

Daughter of Darkness - Victoria - Box Set

Fae Wilds Series
Twist and Turns

Great Temptation Series
The Devil's Footsteps
Heaven's Command
Mortals Surrender

Hidden Secrets Saga
Seventh Mark - Part 1
Seventh Mark - Part 2
Marked By Destiny
Compelled
Fate's Intervention
Chosen Three
The Hidden Secrets Saga: The Complete Series

Kerrigan Chronicles
Stopping Time
A Passage of Time
Ticking Clock
Secrets in Time
Time in the City
Ultimate Future

Kerrigan Memoirs
Chronicles of Devon
Chronicles of Angel
Chronicles of Julian
Chronicles of Molly
Chronicles of Gabriel

Mending Magic Series
Lost Souls
Illusion of Power
Challenging the Dark
Castle of Power
Limits of Magic
Protectors of Light
Mending Magic Box Set Books #1-3

Omega Queen Series
Discipline
Bravery
Courage
Conquer
Strength
Validation
Approval
Blessing
Balance
Grievance
Enchanted

Faking Perfection
The Most Cherished
The Strength to Endure
Royal Factions Box Set Books #1-3

Royal Guard Series
Guardian
Paladin
Sentinel

The Chronicles of Kerrigan
Rae of Hope
Dark Nebula
House of Cards
Royal Tea
Under Fire
End in Sight
Hidden Darkness
Twisted Together
Mark of Fate
Strength & Power
Last One Standing
Rae of Light
The Chronicles of Kerrigan Box Set Books # 1 - 6

The Chronicles of Kerrigan: Gabriel
Living in the Past
Present For Today

Staring at the Future

The Chronicles of Kerrigan Prequel
Christmas Before the Magic
Question the Darkness
Into the Darkness
Fight the Darkness
Alone in the Darkness
Lost in Darkness
The Chronicles of Kerrigan Prequel Series Books #1-3

The Chronicles of Kerrigan Sequel
A Matter of Time
Time Piece
Second Chance
Glitch in Time
Our Time
Precious Time

The Hidden Secrets Saga
Seventh Mark (part 1 & 2)

The Kerrigan Kids
School of Potential
Myths & Magic
Kith & Kin

Playing With Power
Line of Ancestry
Descent of Hope
Illusion of Shadows
Frozen by the Future
Guilt Of My Past
Demise of Magic
Rise of The Prophecy
Deafened By The Past
The Kerrigan Kids Box Set Books #1-3

The Queen's Alpha Series
Eternal
Everlasting
Unceasing
Evermore
Forever
Boundless
Prophecy
Protected
Foretelling
Revelation
Betrayal
Resolved
The Queen's Alpha Box Set

The Senseless Series
Radium Halos - Part 1
Radium Halos - Part 2
Nonsense

Perception
The Senseless - Box Set Books #1-4

Standalone
Shadow of Doubt (Part 1 & 2)
Five Shades of Fantasy
Zwarte Nevel
Shadow of Doubt - Part 1
Shadow of Doubt - Part 2
Four and a Half Shades of Fantasy
Dream Fighter
What Creeps in the Night
Forest of the Forbidden
Arcane Forest: A Fantasy Anthology
The First Fantasy Box Set

Watch for more at www.wjmaybooks.com.

About the Author

About W.J. May

Welcome to USA TODAY BESTSELLING author W.J. May's Page! SIGN UP for W.J. May's Newsletter to find out about new releases, updates, cover reveals and even freebies! http://eepurl.com/97aYf

Website: http://www.wjmaybooks.com

Facebook: http://www.facebook.com/pages/Author-WJ-May-FAN-PAGE/141170442608149?ref=hl *Please feel free to connect with me and share your comments. I love connecting with my readers.* W.J. May grew up in the fruit belt of Ontario. Crazy-happy childhood, she always has had a vivid imagination and loads of energy. After her father passed away in 2008, from a six-year battle with cancer (which she still believes he won the fight against), she began to write again. A passion she'd loved for years, but realized life was too short to keep putting it off. She is a writer of Young Adult, Fantasy Fiction and where ever else her little muses take her.

Read more at www.wjmaybooks.com.

www.ingramcontent.com/pod-product-compliance
Lightning Source LLC
Chambersburg PA
CBHW071610150726
48000CB00004B/1650